'Thank you for a lovely evening,' she said. 'I didn't deserve it, but I enjoyed it immensely.'

'You deserved it,' he said quietly, and, grasping her arms lightly, bent his head and kissed her. While Lissa, dizzy with joy, almost fainted, he let go and stepped back as though he had done something unplanned and regrettable. He said in a slightly embarrassed tone, 'It might be just as well not to mention that we've been out together. You know how hospitals gossip.'

'I'm not about to encourage them to gossip about me,' said Lissa. 'Or you.'

Hugo reached out and ran his fingers through her hair. 'You're a lovely girl, Lissa, and I enjoyed your company tonight. I would enjoy taking you out again some time. . .' there was a heavy pause before he finished '. . .so long as you didn't take it too seriously.

Lissa's heart plunged into her shoes. With some difficulty she managed to remain light and bright as she said, 'I don't take any man very seriously.'

Judith Worthy lives in an outer suburb of Melbourne, Australia, with her husband. When not writing she can usually be found bird-watching or gardening. She also likes to listen to music and the radio, paints a little, likes to travel and is concerned about conservation and animal cruelty. As well as romantic fiction she also writes books for children.

Previous Titles

DOCTOR DARLING
LOCUM LOVER
HEART SPECIALIST

CONDITION CRITICAL

BY

JUDITH WORTHY

MILLS & BOON LIMITED
ETON HOUSE   18–24 PARADISE ROAD
RICHMOND   SURREY   TW9 1SR

*First published in Great Britain 1990
by Mills & Boon Limited*

© Judith Worthy 1990

*Australian copyright 1990
Philippine copyright 1990
This edition 1990*

ISBN 0 263 77077 X

*Set in 10 on 12 pt Linotron Times
03-9012-53613
Typeset in Great Britain by Centracet, Cambridge
Made and printed in Great Britain*

CHAPTER ONE

'ALICIA MORAN, you're crazy!'

It was not the first time during the long flight from London to Melbourne that Lissa had muttered the words. Flinging the book she had been trying to read in her lap, she raked her fingers through the gleaming blonde hair that fell in unruly waves over her shoulders. It was just as well, she thought with a self-mocking twist to her mouth, that the plane was not full and she had three seats to herself. The way she was rabbiting on aloud, anyone alongside her would have thought she was round the twist!

As her family and friends back home did. She felt a pang at the memory of leaving and her eyes misted over as she thought of the farewell party, and then her mother's stoic but reproachful smiles before they'd parted at Heathrow, when she'd murmured, 'I thought you and Phillip were getting along so well. . .'

That had been expected, but Lissa had been unprepared for her father's more perceptive comment in a moment when they were alone. 'I suppose there's some other man, love? Phillip's not the one.'

Their eyes had met and Lissa had tried to keep the truth out of hers, but her father wasn't a man you could fool. He had always been able to sense her feelings. She hoped he wouldn't tell her mother or anyone else.

'Good luck, but don't make a fool of yourself, love,' Jack Moran had said, with a trace of anxiety in his eyes as he squeezed her arm affectionately.

But he was right, she *was* making a fool of herself; there wasn't a hope in hell that anything would come of it. Hugo Stanfield was way out of her sphere. 'I am not going back just because of him,' she insisted to herself yet again, as she flipped the pages of the paperback. 'I happen to like Melbourne and South City General. I happen to like working on the children's ward. I've got a lot of friends. . .'

You've got a lot of friends in London, interrupted her more truthful self, and you could have got a job on a children's ward there if you'd wanted.

'I like Australia,' she muttered emphatically. 'I like the—*weather*!'

She had been having this kind of argument with herself since her return to England after Jacqui's wedding. For some time she had known that she was letting Hugo Stanfield, the new consultant paediatrician, occupy her thoughts and get under her skin more than was good for her, and that unless she wanted her heart broken she had better cut and run.

So she had. But now here she was flying straight back into the very danger she had left. Crazy was the only word for it. There was only one likely outcome— she was going to get hurt. What was more, Dr Hugo Stanfield wasn't even likely to notice. What madness had possessed her to imagine she had a chance with him? Most of the time, for some reason, they had seemed to rub each other up the wrong way, and she was always edgy when he was around.

Lissa sighed deeply and twisted strands of her hair round one finger, making ringlets. Distance always lends enchantment to the scene, she thought, and back in London that had been how it had seemed. She had fooled herself. She had convinced herself that if she had stayed in Melbourne something would have grown between her and Hugo. There was no real evidence for that belief beyond that one time he had taken her out to dinner—the day she'd left the SCG.

If only he hadn't stepped right out of character and treated her to a meal that night, if only he hadn't told her she would be missed—he hadn't actually said *he* would miss her—and if only he hadn't kissed her goodbye—very chastely. . . His niceness had been so unexpected that she'd read more into a kind gesture than she'd had a right to. As a result she'd wished she hadn't been so precipitate about leaving, and had then foolishly beguiled herself into returning to Australia.

She was utterly mad. Hugo wasn't interested in *her*. He probably hadn't even noticed that her hair was naturally blonde, her eyes light brown under silky lashes, and her figure shapely enough for her to be called 'lissom Lissa' by the cheekier young medicos. There were plenty of lissom, lovely young female doctors to attract his attention.

But back in England Phillip Martin, an old school friend she'd run into had noticed her and he'd made it very clear he didn't want her to go gallivanting off to Australia for the second time. If she had any sense, she told herself now, she would have married nice, kind, comfortable Phillip who was doing well in electronics. But Hugo's face had kept intruding every time she thought about marriage to Phillip. Phillip had only made her yearn for Hugo.

She slumped deeper into her seat. Well, it was no good being sensible now, she was almost there. She'd signed on for another two years, so she couldn't change her mind again. And she did like Australia, she reminded herself, she did like the weather and the people and the hospital, and it would be good to see Jacqui and David again. A smile played around her lips—imagine marrying a man called Dr Darling! They were so happy, so madly in love, she thought with wistful envy.

When she'd stayed with Jacqui before the wedding, she hadn't told her about Hugo. There wasn't really anything to tell except that there was this tall, dark consultant paediatrician at South City General whose brooding good looks and deep-toned voice set her limbs trembling, and from whom one of his rare smiles was like a gift from heaven.

'Twenty-four,' Lissa murmued, 'is much too old to have a crush on a doctor. That's for naïvely romantic first-years. What in heaven's name is the matter with me?'

You're getting desperate, that's what, answered her other self with the usual candour. Most of your friends are married and you're not. And let's face it, Hugo is a heart-throb, everyone thinks so. You're just one of many willing to throw themselves at his feet. And you can bet your life he knows it, and takes advantage of it. . .

'Oh, shut up!' Lissa exclaimed, so vehemently that the flight attendant passing paused and asked if she wanted anything.

It had been a long night, with Lissa unable to sleep, and unable to concentrate on reading. She felt exhausted. She asked for a large orange juice. It was nearly breakfast-time anyway, and people were beginning to stir in the aircraft cabin. She lifted the blind and watched the dawn break, looking down at the patterns of red and brown earth below that gradually emerged from the night shadows with an unexpected thrill of pleasure, followed by relief. She *was* glad to be coming back, for other reasons than Hugo.

Maggie Turner was waiting at Tullamarine Airport. 'Lissa!' she yelled as Lissa came through Customs, struggling with a luggage trolley that wanted to go in every direction but straight ahead.

'Maggie!' Lissa ran into a hug from the girl she had been sharing her flat with since Jacqui had left to nurse in the country town where she'd met her Dr Darling. Jacqui had found Maggie as her replacement and no one could have been a more congenial flatmate.

'Great to see you,' said Maggie, looking her over. 'I never thought you'd come back. We must have something after all!' She studied Lissa speculatively as though trying to find the real reason. 'The car's outside—let's get going. I've got the whole day off.'

'Are you sure you want me back at the flat?' Lissa asked anxiously. When she'd left, Maggie had said she wouldn't bother to get anyone else to share. 'Unless it's a fella!' she'd laughed.

'Of course I do! It's been bleak without you, Lissa. I really missed you.' Maggie grinned. 'We had some laughs, didn't we?'

Lissa chuckled. At first she'd thought dark-haired Maggie a bit too ebullient, but the girl's unwavering good nature and sense of humour had complemented her own slightly wry view of life and they had got along splendidly.

It was hot in the sun, with scarcely any breeze. Lissa's skin tingled pleasurably at the sudden warmth after the air-conditioned interior of the terminal. She took a deep breath. Soon she would be swimming and surfing again, enjoying the outdoor life she loved and which, even though Melbourne had a somewhat shorter summer than other places in Australia, was possible for a good part of the year.

'Still on Women's Medical?' she asked as they loaded her luggage into the boot of Maggie's car.

'Yes. But not for much longer.' Maggie straightened up and waved her left hand under Lissa's nose. A small cluster of diamonds sparkled in the sun.

Lissa's mouth fell open. 'You're engaged!'

Maggie feigned reproach. 'Well, don't make it sound as though miracles do happen!'

'Don't be daft! Who? When? Why didn't you tell me when I rang?'

'Who else but the faithful Henry McBride?' said Maggie, going pink. '"When" was Christmas, and I didn't tell you on the phone because you'd have asked too many questions and the call would have cost you a bomb. Besides, I wanted to give you a surprise!'

'Well, you've certainly done that. But I'm thrilled, Maggie. I thought you and Henry were just good friends. You never let on how you felt about him. . .'

Maggie eyed her friend thoughtfully. 'Would you let on how you felt about someone special? It's kind of tempting fate, isn't it? I've been mad about Henry for a couple of years, but I knew he was reluctant to get married again since his first marriage was a failure. This Christmas he suddenly decided to take the plunge.' She laughed. 'I reckon he just got tired of taking his shirts to the launderette and eating take-away pizzas on his own! And I got rewarded for patience!'

Henry McBride was a Scots radiologist at South City General and Lissa liked him a lot. She glanced affec-tionately at Maggie's radiant face, clasped her warmly and kissed her cheek. 'I'm really happy for you both,' she said, meaning it wholeheartedly, while inside her chest a little cold hard lump was forming. Maggie's happiness only increased her own torment. She was crazy to have come back. Talk about chasing a foolish dream!

'So, when we're married, in about six months' time, when Henry can take long service leave, I'll quit nursing,' Maggie said. 'We're going to honeymoon in Scotland.' She sighed happily. 'I can't wait. . .mountains, moors and real castles! And men in kilts playing bagpipes. . .'

'You won't see too many of those in the streets,' Lissa cautioned, laughing.

Lissa started work almost immediately. As usual, the hospital was short-staffed and the children's wards were busy. There had been some changes in staff since she had left some weeks before Christmas, but a few familiar faces greeted her. Warren Barker, the charge nurse on the children's surgical ward which was known as Pinocchio, sounded genuinely pleased to see her back.

'We'll have to marry you off to one of our medicos,' he suggested with a grin, 'and then maybe you'll stay for keeps.'

'I might leave and have lots of babies to give you more work than ever,' she joked.

Father of three Warren laughed loudly. 'Shall I send a memo round?' he teased. 'We've got a new intake of interns, you know.'

'Too young for me,' said Lissa, wrinkling her nose. There's only one person I want it sent to, she thought dreamily, then shook herself in annoyance. She must get Hugo Stanfield out of her system, not moon over him. She exchanged a few more bantering words, then went back to her duties on the ward.

Three days later she had not seen Hugo, but hesitated to ask where he was for fear of giving herself away. She had expected someone to mention him, but no one did. A couple of doctors she knew came on rounds, but never the consultant. Could he have gone to another hospital? The thought of that opened a void in her stomach, and try as she might she could not regard the possibility as a good thing. She had to see him and work with him if she was to get over her silly crush on the man. She had to see him to convince herself that what she felt was not even the beginnings of love.

Fortunately, the children she nursed distracted her most of the time, so that Hugo only haunted her dreams. He wasn't her type, she kept telling herself. She didn't go for the too-good-to-be-true sort of male good looks, and if the past was any indication she was much more inclined to fall for ugly ducklings or gangling misfits than arrogant eyebrow-lifting consultants. He was the sort of man she avoided. He was probably very conceited and very boring.

Towards the end of her first week back at South City General, Lissa had begun to convince herself that Hugo Stanfield must have left. She eventually took courage and asked Karyn Wentworth, who had been on the ward with her before, about him. They were tidying up after having settled the younger children down for their afternoon nap.

'I haven't seen Dr Stanfield since I came back,' Lissa

remarked casually as she propped a well-loved Cabbage Patch doll on a small patient's bedside locker. 'Isn't he with us any more?'

Karyn was bending over a little girl who was fast asleep. She was Asian, with jet-black hair, and smooth olive skin. 'Isn't she beautiful?' Karyn said. 'Look at her eyelashes. . .she's like a little doll!' She glanced up at Lissa. 'Hugo? Yes, of course he's still with us. Didn't you know? He went to the States just after Christmas, to attend some conference on SIDS, I gather. I forget how long he's supposed to be away.'

Lissa drew in a sharp involuntary breath. She knew that Hugo was deeply involved in research into Sudden Infant Death Syndrome, or cot death as it was often called. He had been responsible for setting up the research unit at the hospital.

Karyn grinned. 'You've had a bellyful of old Crossthwaite too, have you? Haven't we all?' She rolled her eyes. 'At least Hugo's good with the kids, even if he does ignore the staff.'

Lissa was surprised to find herself defending the absent paediatrician. 'I don't think he means to be offhand. It's just his manner. He's a bit reserved.'

'Well, you should know,' said Karyn with a meaningful look. 'I gather he took you out to dinner before you left.'

'How do you know that?' Lissa was dismayed.

'You were seen, Lissa. I forget who. Wait a minute, I think it was Paul—Paul Norris. He was a bit keen on you, wasn't he? I guess he was jealous seeing you with Hugo.' She cocked an eyebrow curiously. 'Don't tell me Hugo is why you came back?'

Lissa was horrified. Karyn was the last person she wanted to guess how stupid she was. She tried to stop the tide of scarlet that threatened to suffuse her face. 'Karyn, really! He had nothing to do that night, and I happened to run into him as I was leaving, and he offered me a lift and then suggested a meal as a sort of—farewell. As for Paul,' she rushed on, anxious to switch the subject, 'I haven't seen him either since I came back. What's happened to him?'

'Nothing drastic. He's on holiday, that's all. Surfing in Sydney. He doesn't know you're back?'

'No.'

'I thought you might have kept in touch,' Karyn probed slyly.

Lissa shrugged. 'There was nothing between us, Karyn. Paul's nice and I went out with him a few times, but not seriously.'

Karyn straightened the covers on another cot and stood up. 'Well, I for one will be glad to see both of them back. Anything's better than a surfeit of Crossthwaite. I don't know why he doesn't retire. He's the bane of every nurse's existence. And the children think he's an ogre.'

'He doesn't understand today's youngsters, I suppose,' Lissa commented. She had more than once moped up a few tears after one of the crusty old consultant's stern lectures to a young patient who had been larking about during his round. After Hugo's arrival he had visited the wards less and less, and had been none too pleased to be obliged to during Hugo's absence.

Lissa went through the remainder of her shift with mixed feelings. One minute she felt so light-headed she felt she was walking on air, the next so leaden her feet felt nailed to the floor. She tried to pretend it was because she was looking forward to seeing Paul Norris again, but the truth was she had hardly given the young red-haired registrar a second thought since her return. Like poor Phillip back in London, he wasn't Hugo.

Next morning Lissa was late as a result of her tram losing power for a time, and then becoming stuck in a traffic jam. Rushing out of the nurses' room still pinning her security tag on to her crisp white uniform dress, she did not see the figure in the corridor until she almost collided with him.

'Steady on!' Strong hands gripped her upper arms and for a moment her nose was perilously close to the white coat in front of it. A fraction of a second before he spoke she knew who it was. The faint drift of his aftershave was, she realised, something she had never been consciously aware of, but now her subconscious remembered and associated. She lifted her face just as he exclaimed. 'Lissa!' Or had he only said 'Sister'?

The blood rushed to her head. 'H-hello.' Her voice shook and her knees threatened to buckle under her. 'You're back.' How idiotic she sounded!

'*You're* back,' he emphasised. 'I thought you said you were going home for good?' He seemed suddenly aware that he was holding her arms and abruptly let go. The dark eyes looked for an answer. 'Why?' A lock of hair had fallen characteristically across his forehead and he smoothed it back.

His impact was as potent as ever, and Lissa stepped back a pace. She could hardly say, 'Because of you.' She tried to throw off the fact of her return nonchalantly. 'Oh, I liked it here more than I thought, I suppose.'

One dark eyebrow angled slightly. 'Winter in London can be a bit depressing.' A faint smile curled one corner of his mouth. 'Found yourself longing for the sunshine, I suppose.'

'Other things too,' she said boldly, while her insides threatened total melt-down. 'As my flatmate said, Australia must have something after all!'

It was both agony and bliss to walk with him along the short strip of corridor to the wards. Smiling more openly than she'd ever known him to before, he held open one of the double ward doors for her, and she heard herself saying, 'Did you have a successful trip? I heard you'd been to a SIDS conference in America.' She tried not to sound too interested.

A grim look instantly replaced his smile. 'It was illuminating, but also frustrating. We're no nearer the solution. There are as many theories as researchers, it seems.' His frown lines had deepened and Lissa felt immediate sympathy.

He paused outside Warren Barker's office, lifted a hand and dropped it casually on her shoulder. The touch electrified her. He was affecting her now much worse than he had before. She had thought about him so much, and then, encountering him so unexpectedly, she had been plunged into utter confusion.

'Well, it's nice to see you back. I'm sure the SCG is grateful. Good nurses are precious.' The glimmer of a half-formed smile was fleetingly back again. He actually sounded as though *he* was pleased to see her, Lissa thought, and immediately rejected the possibility. He was just being polite, for heaven's sake!

As he turned to go into the charge nurse's office, the door opened and Warren appeared. 'Oh—Hugo, I was hoping you'd come down today. I'd like your advice about a three-year-old we admitted last night. . .' He paused. 'Good morning, Lissa.' He was running his

fingers through his bushy brown hair in typical Warren
Barker style, and looking hassled as usual too.

'Sorry I'm late,' she apologised. 'My tram lost power,
and there was a traffic jam.'

Warren seemed uninterested in her excuse, so she
hurried away. She was about to go through the door
into the main ward when it was flung open and for the
second time in minutes she almost collided with
another white-coated figure. This one too exclaimed,
'Lissa!' Only she was certain this time that he had used
her name.

'Paul. . .' It was too soon after seeing Hugo. And
the contrast made this encounter anticlimactic. 'Did
you have a good holiday?'

'Great. . .but get you! I never thought you'd come
back. What happened?' His hazel eyes twinkled under
the thatch of ginger hair, and although his slightly
crooked nose and lopsided grin were endearing, Lissa
felt like a balloon that had just been pricked. He placed
his hands on her shoulders and pulled her close. 'Did
you miss me after all?' Before she could escape he had
bent and kissed her, briefly but passionately.

Lissa pulled back. 'Paul!' Guiltily she glanced over
her shoulder, and was mortified to see that Hugo was
still there. A phone was ringing and Warren was just
disappearing into his office and not looking their way,
but Hugo's gaze had definitely taken in the touching
little scene before he quickly averted his eyes and
strode after the charge nurse.

'I'll be in trouble now,' said Lissa. 'He saw us!'

Paul Norris flung his arm around her. 'So what? I
can welcome back one of our best and most beautiful
nurses, can't I?'

'Nobody else has done it your way!' She was sure he

had acted deliberately because Hugo was watching, but it was hard to stay annoyed with him. 'And I really must get to work, Paul. I'm awfully late already.'

He detained her a moment longer. 'How about dinner tonight?'

Lissa hesitated. Paul's enthusiastic kiss had made her wary. She hoped he wasn't really labouring under the illlusion that she had come back because she found him irresistible after all. Well, if he was, she would soon make her position clear, and if he wasn't offended maybe it would do her good to go out with him anyway. Pual might help her to get her feet back on the ground.

'Well, if you're not doing anything. . .'

'I might have to cancel the Governor-General!' he returned sunnily. 'You're back with Maggie Turner?' When she nodded, he arranged to pick her up at seven-thirty. 'I'm not on call tonight,' he said with relief, 'so we can enjoy a whole evening without interruption.'

Lissa found herself having slight misgivings about that.

CHAPTER TWO

'IT WORKS!' Karyn Wentworth sailed jubilantly into the nurses' room where Lissa was grabbing a quick cup of coffee, and skipped to the coffee machine.

'What does?' Lissa set aside the nursing journal she had been glancing through. She hadn't been reading it because her mind was too preoccupied, not with Hugo for once, but with a small patient who had been admitted that morning, and who worried her greatly.

'Voodoo!'

'Voodoo? I thought you were on to some new piece of high-tech equipment. What are you talking about, Karyn?'

'Dr Crossthwaite. And not voodoo exactly. I mean, I didn't stick pins in a doll or anything, I just put a mild hex on the old boy and willed him to retire. Warren just told me that he finally has!'

Lissa laughed. 'You're a witch!' She pushed a couple of pins up into the smooth chignon in which she wore her hair for work, and tucked a stray curl behind her ear.

Karyn flopped down beside her on the couch. 'Actually I feel quite eerie, even though I don't really believe in all that rubbish. I just chanted "retire, Crossthwaite, retire" every night before I went to sleep and sent him vibrations!'

'Coincidence, that's all,' Lissa reassured.

'Hmm. Makes you wonder, though.' Karyn delved into the biscuit jar and grabbed a handful. Speaking with a mouth full of ginger nut, she said thoughtfully, 'Maybe it would work in other ways. For instance—I wonder who I could make fall in love with me. . .' She grinned wickedly. 'You'd need to be careful, though. You might get more than you could handle. How about handsome Dr Stanfield? He's not married, is he?'

It was only a joke, but Lissa's heart turned over. 'I've never heard anything about a wife.'

'I heard a rumour that he's divorced, but he's not the sort to discuss his private life. Maybe it was only a rumour. Perhaps he's just a good-time guy. It'd be a challenge, though. . .' Karyn's eyes sparkled mischievously.

Lissa said nothing. She was digesting the possibility that Hugo might be divorced, might have been married once. She didn't think, whether he had or not, that he would qualify as a good-time guy. Still, you never knew. Some men were dark horses.

Karyn tossed her head. 'Well, anyway, I don't think I'll bother, it probably wouldn't be worth the effort. He's probably as immune to spells as he is to nurses who might presume to put one on him. I reckon the competition would be too tough anyway.'

'Competition?' queried Lissa.

'There are too many female doctors around these days. We poor nurses don't stand a chance,' moaned Karyn. 'Look at Dr Rossney. No one has a right to be that beautiful and have brains as well.'

Jayne Rossney was a newcomer, an intern, who distracted every pair of male eyes in the hospital. She was tall and willowy, with straight dark hair and patrician good looks. Her deep blue eyes had a sharply critical gaze and, as did most of the other nurses, Lissa felt unaccountably diminished when talking to her. She wasn't unpleasant, but she had a naturally superior air. With other doctors, however, she was quite different, and when she was speaking, or laughing, it was obvious how riveted their attention was. Lissa hadn't failed to notice that Hugo Stanfield was as rapt as anyone.

'Well, she won't need to resort to witchcraft to get a man,' she commented drily.

'Neither will some others I could mention,' said Karyn, jumping up and giving Lissa a meaningful look. 'Have you taken up with Paul Norris again?'

'I had dinner with him the other night,' Lissa admitted. 'And we're going to Lorne at the weekend, surfing.' She rose too, her break over. 'With a group,' she added. People were too anxious to pair others off. 'We're just friends with the same sporting interests.'

'Good friends often become lovers,' said Karyn, leading the way out. 'And then they get married or live together or whatever.'

'Not Paul and me,' Lissa emphasised. She had made it quite clear to Paul that she enjoyed his company but was not likely to become serious about him, either to marry him or live with him. He had accepted that, saying he wasn't ready to settle down and raise a family yet, nor did he want an exclusive relationship.

As they went back to the ward, Lissa could not help voicing the concern over a patient that had been troubling her. 'What do you think of young Toby?' she asked.

Karyn looked at her narrowly. 'I don't know, Lissa. It's too easy to jump to conclusions. Maybe he did fall down some steps. . .kids break their arms all the time.'

'I gather this is the third time he's been in,' Lissa said. 'I know some kids are accident-prone, but there's something about poor little Toby, the way he clings when you give him a cuddle, as though no one else ever does. . .and his mother has that sullen, evasive look.'

Karyn paused, frowning. 'I know what you're thinking and it's crossed my mind too, but we must be careful, Lissa, not to—to make accusations. We could be wrong.'

'His father never comes to see the boy,' Lissa pointed out.

'That doesn't mean anything.'

Lissa's face was grim. 'We see it, Karyn, we *know*, and we can't do anything about it. . .that's what makes me so angry. If someone's beating up that poor little kid. . .' Tears of helpless anger flashed into her eyes. 'He's barely three years old!'

'Take it easy,' Karyn said gently. 'Don't get emotional. We can do something. Warren will alert Welfare if he feels there's a need.'

Lissa forced herself to calm down. 'Sorry, I didn't mean to get all worked up about it. He's such a brave little kid, so trusting. You can jab a needle into him and he doesn't turn a hair, never cries. Those big brown eyes just stare at you as though trying to tell you something.'

'He's a pretty quiet child all round,' observed Karyn. 'Doesn't talk much yet.' She added, 'Are you doing the round with Hugo today?'

'Yes.' Lissa felt the usual tightening in her stomach at the prospect. However hard she tried, the appearance of Dr Stanfield was guaranteed to send every rational thought flying out of her mind, and impair her ability to concentrate. If she was the nurse designated to assist when Hugo did a round of the wards, only the presence of Charge Nurse Barker prevented her from making a fool of herself. It was getting worse, not better.

Warren buttonholed her a few minutes after she'd left Karyn. 'Lissa. . .look, Hugo's going to be late this morning, and I've got to go to an urgent conference with the DN over staffing levels. You can cope, can't you?'

Lissa could only say, 'Yes, of course.' But the moment his back was turned she bit her lip and wished she could faint, or sprain her ankle or find some pretext to renege. Doing the round with Hugo alone would be an ordeal. Although, with at least one of the registrars there, she wouldn't be entirely alone with him.

Warren hadn't said how late the consultant was going to be, so for the next hour Lissa was in torment waiting for him to arrive. Every time the ward doors opened her heart raced crazily. She kept glancing at her watch. If he didn't come soon he was going to clash with lunch. Maybe he wasn't going to come at all. Relief and disappointment merged, and then all at once there he was, striding towards her as she walked up and down soothing a toddler who was recovering from otitis media but was still suffering some discomfort as well as missing his mother.

'Good morning, Lissa,' Hugo said briskly, then, 'What's up with this little chap?'

'He's the otitis media. Andrew.'

'Ah, yes. How are those Grommet tubes we inserted functioning? Perhaps I'd better take a look.'

Lissa said, 'I think he's just missing his mum. She's got three other children and she can't stay overnight with him.' She smiled, half apologetically. 'I thought a bit of a cuddle would help to settle him.'

'Which it apparently has,' Hugo remarked. He

smiled at the now silent Andrew, who had lifted his head from Lissa's shoulder to watch him with huge interested dark eyes. 'You're a lucky young fellow, do you know that, Andrew? A lot of people would like to be cuddled by Sister.'

To her horror, Lissa blushed. 'You—er—know Warren's had to go to a meeting?'

'Yes.'

Lissa had expected Paul or Dr Rossney to be with him and she looked questioningly towards the doors. 'Isn't anyone else. . .?' Consultants didn't usually visit patients without the regular doctors in tow, especially interns.

'Not today,' he said. 'The schedule's been thrown out of gear. I'm pushed for time myself.' His dark eyes met hers with an intensity that set every nerve tingling.

Lissa wondered why he hadn't cancelled the visit. It wasn't vital.

'Then we'd better start,' she said. 'Do you want to examine Andrew first?'

He nodded briefly. 'It might be necessary to prescribe some nasal drops to help the drainage.'

'I'll just fetch the trolley,' said Lissa. 'It's all ready.'

She put the now quieter Andrew back in his cot, and sped off to get the examination trolley and case notes. Hugo was talking reassuringly to a small patient recovering from an eye injury when she returned.

He looked steadily at her and remarked, 'You never used to scuttle about like a startled deer.'

Lissa blushed again. 'I'm sorry.'

'You don't have to be anxious because Warren's not here.'

She lifted her chin. 'I'm not.'

She sat on a chair and held the toddler on her lap,

clasping him firmly, so that Hugo could easily examine his ear. Hugo was swift and thorough, and very gentle. Andrew whimpered a little but did not struggle.

Handing back the auriscope, Hugo said, 'Fine. . .it looks just fine.' His eyes met Lissa's briefly. 'You were probably right, he's just missing his mum.'

They moved swiftly from patient to patient, and to Lissa's surprise her nervousness at being alone with him quickly disappeared. Instead, she had a new feeling of co-operation, of sharing a task with him, and that brought her an inner glow. He wasn't rubbing her up the wrong way today. He was treating her as a person of intelligence with opinions worth listening to, just as though she were the nurse in charge, which officially she was in Warren's absence. She began to enjoy the round in a way she had not experienced before.

Pausing before one child's cot, he suddenly said, 'No regrets about coming back?'

'No.' It was true and yet not true. She wasn't sure how she felt.

'You were certainly warmly welcomed by one admirer.'

Lissa flinched. She knew he was referring to Paul's spontaneous kiss in the corridor which he had witnessed. He had evidently not mentioned it to Warren, who was the kind to disapprove of intimacies between staff when on duty and would have taken her to task over it.

'Dr Norris was very surprised to see me,' Lissa explained, meeting his eyes bravely. 'He is sometimes rather impulsive.'

'A trait that needs to be discouraged in doctors,' Hugo advised, moving to their next patient.

He had seemed to smile, but she couldn't be sure whether he was teasing her or reprimanding her. It was almost more unnerving when he smiled than when he didn't. His smile was rarely more than a muscular shift, with no warmth reflected in his eyes. Thick lashes almost conealed them most of the time, and even when he was looking directly at you they were always shadowed, giving him an air of detachment.

With the children, his aloofness was less noticeable. He seemed able to come down to their level and meet them on equal terms. He was never patronising and seemed to have an instinctive understanding of the apprehensions of young people in hospital, especially for the first time. He was considerate towards parents too, always patient and unhurried when they stopped him to ask questions. If they noticed that he seemed a little preoccupied, they probably thought as everyone else did that it was because he was a busy man, taking his responsibilities very seriously. Lissa sometimes felt it was more than that. Even having dinner with him had not allowed her to penetrate his reserve. Hugo Stanfield was a very private person indeed.

He had come from the West—Perth—and nobody knew much about him. Even Paul had not dared to ask whether he was divorced, as was rumoured. Perhaps it was this very aloofness that made him intriguing, Lissa thought, that made him attractive. Like Heathcliff in *Wuthering Heights*, like Mr Rochester in *Jane Eyre* and a dozen other romantic heroes. . .

'. . .and which one did Dr Rossney prescribe for Emily?' Hugo's voice suddenly cut into Lissa's wandering thoughts and she realised in dismay that she had not heard all of what he had said.

Momentarily she was fazed. She looked at him

blankly, transfixed by the deep brown colour of his eyes which were looking steadily at her, waiting for her to answer.

A moment later she was shocked to hear a velvety female voice giving the answer, but it wasn't her own. She turned quickly. Dr Jayne Rossney was behind them. Jayne greeted Hugo with a smiling 'Good morning, Hugo,' but had only a cursory nod for Lissa. Hugo returned the greeting, and it seemed to Lissa that his eyes lingered far longer on Jayne's face than they ever had on hers.

He said, 'Ah, Jayne, I'm glad you managed to come along. There seems to be some mild reaction here. I think maybe you should try an alternative antibiotic. Emily's temperature is still a little high and there's slight furring of the tongue.'

Lissa noticed the swift pursing of Jayne Rossney's lips at this implied criticism, but Hugo evidently did not. He had turned to the child and was saying, 'Poke your tongue out at Dr Rossney.' Emily needed no encouragement.

The two doctors had moved away from Lissa, who stood at the foot of the bed feeling eclipsed. They were discussing the patient in low voices, and Lissa's former warm feeling vanished. For a little while she had fooled herself that there was a new kind of rapport between them, albeit only a professional one, but now it was plain that even that was merely wishful thinking. Before her was real rapport. Two doctors discussing a patient on equal footing. She could never do that. Was there also personal rapport between them? she wondered. Did they meet off duty? There was a closeness about the two figures that suggested they were companionable. Or was she exaggerating it because she was jealous?

For the remainder of the round Lissa kept a polite distance and was stiffly co-operative when needed to provide information or to hold or distract a child to facilitate examination. The more she looked at Jayne Rossney, the more she believed it was just a matter of time before those two fell in love, if they weren't already. Hadn't she known it? She had no chance whatever with a man like Hugo Stanfield. Even if nobody knew about it, she was making an absolute fool of herself.

Why can't he fall in love with me? she thought, trailing after them miserably. Why can't I *make* him? On the tail of the question came the memory of Karyn's successful hexing of Dr Crossthwaite and her joking remark about the possibility of the same method being used to make someone fall in love with her. Appalled at herself, Lissa suddenly found her brain chanting, 'Let him fall in love with me, not her—love me, not her, love me, not her.' And as her eyes bored deliberately into the back of his pristine white coat, she wasn't even laughing. When he turned suddenly and looked hard at her for a moment before speaking, she felt her colour rising guiltily and quickly looked away.

After Hugo and Jayne had finished seeing all the patients, they stood quietly talking in the corridor while Lissa returned the case notes to the charge nurse's office. She was about to leave when Hugo's large frame filled the doorway. He came in and pulled the door to.

'What time is Warren back?' he asked.

'I don't know. He didn't say.'

'I'll hang on for a while,' said Hugo, consulting his watch. 'Like to get me a cup of coffee? I shan't have time for lunch today.'

'Would you like me to have some sandwiches sent

up? You shouldn't go without lunch. . .' Lissa broke off. It was no business of hers to nag him about health.

'All right, but I mightn't have time to eat them.' He sank into a chair and propped his feet on the desk. He looked weary, Lissa suddenly thought, as though he hadn't had much sleep lately. She hurried out, angry with herself for wondering if Jayne Rossney was responsible.

While the kettle was boiling, she rang for sandwiches. She took the mug of coffee into the office and found Hugo with his head sunk on his chest, hands interlinked across his diaphragm, as though fast asleep. But he wasn't. He roused at the slight sound she made entering, and sat up.

'That was quick. Thanks.'

'Your sandwiches are on their way,' she told him.

'Thanks again. You're very efficient, Sister.'

Was he being sarcastic? 'It doesn't take much organisational ability to order coffee and sandwiches,' she said tersely, realising that she was letting him rile her for the first time that day.

She turned to go, but he detained her. 'Stay for a minute. . .'

She hesitated. Why did he want her to stay? 'The children's lunches will be here,' she said. 'I have to help.'

'Five minutes,' he said, and gestured to another chair.

Lissa sat, wondering. The silly chant was still echoing in the back of her brain. Just as well he couldn't read her mind! She waited, looking at him. Surely it wasn't working already? Had he felt compelled to ask her to stay without knowing why? Was he being subconsciously motivated by her magic? She almost giggled at the thought.

'Did you work while you were back in England?'
Hugo asked finally. 'Or did you take a holiday?'

'I worked for a few weeks. Just agency jobs.'

'And then decided you'd rather nurse here?'

She nodded. She was sure he didn't really want to
know, but she went on, 'I suppose I had to go back to
find out that I really preferred being here.'

'A lot of migrants do that.' He eyed her speculatively. 'I expect you'll be torn between the two countries
forever now. Wherever you are, you'll be homesick for
the other place.'

'Perhaps.' Lissa felt uncomfortable talking about
herself. She said, 'The SIDS Counselling Unit is functioning well. It was obviously needed. I suppose you
got some fresh ideas when you were in the US?'

'Some useful information, yes. What we need,
though, is more money for research.'

'Last year's Red Nose Day raised a substantial
amount,' Lissa reminded him.

A faint chuckle escaped the otherwise grim lips.
'You looked sensational in your red nose, as I recall.'

'Didn't we all? The children loved it too. It was good
to see everyone joining in. Nobody minded looking
silly for a good cause.' She paused and then asked,
'How long do you think it will be before there's a
definitive answer, before we know how to prevent cot
deaths?'

He looked at her for a long moment and there were
conflicting emotions in his face. 'Too long.'

There was a sudden quietness in the room and Lissa
felt his frustration strongly. There could be few puzzles
in medicine so great as sudden infant death syndrome,
for which it seemed there might be many possible
causes. His own inability to find definitive answers

must be a burden. Perhaps that, more than anything, accounted for his air of gloomy preoccupation.

Lissa would have given anything to be able to stay and continue the conversation, anything just to be there with him, but the rattle of trolleys heralded the arrival of lunch. Reluctantly, she jumped up. 'I must go.' As she spoke there was a knock and she opened the door to an auxiliary bearing a plate of sandwiches. She took them and placed them in front of Hugo. 'More coffee?'

'No, thanks, this'll do.' He reached for a sandwich. 'Thanks, Lissa. I'll just hang on while I eat these in case Warren comes back.'

Lissa went out, still slightly bemused. For the consultant paediatrician to be lunching in the charge nurse's office was unusual, not to say peculiar. That he had detained her to talk about nothing of specific relevance to her job was even odder. But to imagine that he had been compelled against his will to do it, that witchcraft, even the white kind, actually worked, was ludicrous. Still, Dr Crossthwaite *had* retired. . .

Lissa lay in bed that night feeling utterly ashamed of herself. What a pathetic thing to do, to try and will a man to fall in love with you! She deserved to be punished for it, and probably would be. Resolutely she put such nonsense out of her mind, but to her dismay discovered it was only temporarily banished. Like a virus that hangs on and on, the words clung to her subconscious. Love me, not Jayne, love me, not Jayne.

The words were still there next day, becoming now like a millstone, and no matter how scornfully she mocked herself they wouldn't go away. No matter how often she told herself that it was a load of old rubbish, and there was no way in the world you could influence a person by willing them to do your bidding, a crazy corner of her mind insisted that it might just work.

The funny thing was that when Hugo suddenly appeared unexpectedly she wasn't even thinking about him—not consciously anyway. She was alone in the little room where mothers fed their babies, giving a bottle feed to a very young baby whose mother could not be there all the time during the day. The door was open, and a shadow blocking the natural light made her glance up. Hugo stood there, looking at her with that tantalising half smile on his lips. She felt the same emotional jolt as she always did. Her pulse quickened and yet at the same time she felt antipathy. Love/hate, she thought. I love him, but I hate him too for not loving me.

He strolled in, quirking an eyebrow at her. 'You look very maternal.'

For some reason she felt vulnerable, sitting there holding a baby, with his large frame looming over her. It wasn't much better, though, when he propped himself against the edge of the changing table. There was an almost palpable masculine aura about the man that was disconcerting to say the least.

'I don't know that I am! With the size family we have here, one can have too much of a good thing.'

'Do you come from a large family?'

'By today's standards, I suppose I do. I've got four brothers and sisters. I'm in the middle.' She laughed. 'It usually meant, and still does, in the middle of the arguments.'

'I dare say you'll be wanting children of your own one of these days?'

The directness of the question surprised her, so she answered a little flippantly. 'Well, I guess it's not regarded as essential these days, but I'd rather like to get married first.' Then she blushed deeply. What a thing to say!

'A nice old-fashioned girl, are you?' There was a hint of mockery in his tone.

'Not old-fashioned exactly, just in favour of stable family life.' It was an odd conversation, she thought. He seemed edgy and she felt uncomfortable. He'd never quizzed her on personal matters before. Even that night he'd taken her to dinner they'd talked mainly about hospitals, the one where she'd trained, which he knew, and the SCG.

'Is that what you had?' he asked.

'Very much so. We have very loving parents.'

'You must miss your family, surely? Didn't they try and persuade you not to come back?'

They were approaching the danger zone. Lissa said, 'Yes, they did, and of course I miss them, but. . .' She concentrated on the baby for a moment before saying, 'My parents expect all of us children to live our own lives.' The baby finished the feed and Lissa set the bottle aside. She wiped his milky lips gently, then held him against her shoulder, while lightly massaging his back.

'He's coming along very nicely, isn't he?' she remarked, since Hugo still seemed disposed to stay. The baby had recently undergone an operation for an intestinal obstruction and was now almost ready to go home. As the mother had other children to care for, Hugo had suggested that a few extra days in hospital would relieve her of constant nursing care.

'Splendidly.' His eyes met hers in an odd searching way as though there was something he wanted to say but wasn't too sure what it was himself.

The baby had been winded a couple of times and now drooped against Lissa's shoulder. 'I think I'd better put this young man down for a nap,' she said.

She started to get up, but the chair was a low one, and as she rose unsteadily, Hugo moved swiftly to help her. For a moment she was standing with his hands on her arms, the baby between them, and his eyes boring into hers in the most alarming manner. Then he abruptly looked away and let go of her, stepping back with that slightly nonplussed look again as though he'd caught himself doing something he didn't want to, but had felt compelled to do.

Lissa murmured, 'Thanks,' and fussed with the gown of her small charge. He hadn't said why he was there, so she asked, 'Is there anything I can do for you?'

He seemed surprised at the question, lost for a reply for a moment, then he said, 'I was just passing.'

Lissa's heart gave a guilty lurch. Had he really felt compelled to come and see her? Was he really looking a little nonplussed? Perhaps she wasn't imagining it after all. Torn between horror and happiness, she searched her mind for something intelligent to say, a topic for a conversation that would show him that he and she had loads of things in common after all.

And then he ruined it by saying, 'Is Warren around?'

Lissa came down off her cloud. He hadn't come to see her—what a daft idea! 'I expect he's at lunch,' she said, trying to keep the tremor out of her voice.

As she walked out of the door ahead of him, she said, 'I'll tell Warren you wanted him.'

'No, don't bother. It wasn't important.' He turned quickly as though anxious to be away and strode along the corridor.

Lissa settled Timothy in his cot, her mind in a whirl.

She was practically sure now that Hugo hadn't come to see Warren, that it was an excuse. But if he hadn't, why had he come when he wasn't expected? To see her? No, that was crazy. She was getting things out of all proportion. There was no such thing as hexing people or willing people to do what you wanted. She didn't believe such rubbish. She'd stopped doing it anyway.

But as she tucked Timothy up, the chant surfaced mockingly. Love me, not Jayne, love me, not Jayne. You can't make someone love you, she told herself, so stop being an idiot. You're round the twist, so besotted you'll believe anything, clutch at any straw. Grow up, for heaven's sake, and come to your senses. Hugo Stanfield is never going to fall in love with you.

By the time she finished her shift that afternoon, Lissa had knocked a little sense into her brain and was concentrating her whole mind on getting ready for a weekend off. Paul was off too, and they were going to learn windsurfing, a sport she had long wanted to try. But first she had some grocery shopping to do. It was her turn, and when she'd checked that morning the cupboard had been almost bare.

The supermarket was crowded with Friday shoppers and Lissa ended up with more bags than she could comfortably carry even the short distance to the block of flats. She decided she'd better call a cab. She lugged her bags to the red phone, where several people were waiting ahead of her, and looked in her purse for coins, muttering under her breath when she found she had no appropriate silver left. There was a sweets kiosk a few metres away, so she gathered up her bags to go and get some change.

'You're a bit loaded up; can I help?' The voice at

her side was deep-toned and familiar, and totally unexpected. What on earth was Hugo Stanfield doing in a supermarket?'

'What are you doing here?' she blurted.

'Weekend shopping like you, I presume,' he said. He was carrying two carrier bags. At her look of surprise, he added, 'I have to eat too, you know.'

'Yes, but I thought. . .' What had she thought? That someone of his eminence would have someone to do his shopping for him? She felt foolish. 'I just hadn't imagined you wheeling a trolley around a supermarket, I suppose,' she said lamely.

'I dare say there are a lot of things you haven't imagined me doing,' he suggested, with that tiny glimmer of a smile that tilted his lips but never entered his eyes.

'It's hard sometimes to think of hospital people in their other lives,' she confessed. 'You tend to think of them in the role they're in there as a twenty-four-hours-a-day one.'

'But you do different things out of uniform.'

'Yes. . .'

He relented. 'Well, you're right, I don't often shop in supermarkets, but my housekeeper forgot a few items and I said I'd pick them up on my way home.'

'That was considerate of you.'

He looked at her as though suspecting she was taking the mickey. 'Well, let's not stand here dissecting it,' he said briskly. 'Let me help you to your car with those bags.'

'I haven't got a car.'

He studied her for a moment. 'Ah, yes, I remember, you travel by tram. Well, then, I'd better give you a lift. You won't be popular on a tram with all this.'

'My flat's walking distance from here,' Lissa reminded him. 'I only use the tram to get to work. I was going to ring a cab as I'd bought rather more than I intended, but I'd run out of change. . .'

He switched both his carriers to one hand and was gathering up some of hers with the other. 'If you can manage those two, I'll take the rest.'

'No, really,' she protested. 'I can get a cab.'

'Are you at the same flat where you were living before?'

'Yes.'

'Well, it won't take a minute to drive you there,' he insisted. 'Come on.'

Lissa ceased protesting. She let him drive her home and help her up to the flat with the groceries.

'Thank you for going out of your way,' she said, but he cut off her thanks.

'I haven't. I don't live very far away—Rosewood Avenue.'

Lissa hadn't known that, but she was hardly surprised. Rosewood Avenue was a well-known street, not far away in a rather more affluent area. Once he was inside her flat, she felt obliged to offer him a cup of coffee which he accepted. He seemed in no hurry to go. Strange little shivers were circling round inside her.

'Where's your flatmate?' he asked.

'Maggie's on the middle shift. We don't see much of each other lately.'

'Are you going out tonight?'

She had answered truthfully before she thought about it. 'No.'

'Have dinner with me?' One eyebrow was half raised at her.

'I'm not leaving the country,' she said lightly, hiding her surprise. 'I don't need a farewell gesture.'

'What about a welcome back one?'

Lissa suddenly panicked. What had she brought on herself? This was precisely what she had dreamed about, Hugo asking her out again, and yet she was nervous of accepting now it had happened. And all because of that silly magic nonsense of Karyn's. What if she got more than she bargained for? What if Hugo really was only a good-time guy? What if he had sensed that she was attracted to him and his ego was telling him to take advantage of it. Oh, what a muddle! she thought; here I am with what I want within reach and I'm afraid to take it.

'I'm sorry,' she said, 'but I'm going away for the weekend. I've got rather a lot to do and I want to go to bed early.' Instantly she regretted the words. What was the matter with her, passing up an evening out with Hugo, an evening that could be the start of something?

He stood up. His face showed nothing of his thoughts. 'With Dr Norris?' The question was sharp.

'And a few other people. We're going to learn windsurfing.'

'I'm sure that will be fun,' he said, as though it was the last thing he would have considered as fun himself. 'Well, I'd better let you get on with it. Thanks for the coffee.'

She saw him to the door. 'Thanks for the lift, Hugo.'

'You're welcome,' he said, but his voice was stiff with the disappointment of a man who had been rebuffed.

Lissa closed the door and leaned on it, grinding her teeth. She yanked her hair down about her face and raked her fingers through it. She was nuts, that was what, plain ordinary nuts. She'd had the man here and she'd let him go. All because she'd suddenly got cold feet.

CHAPTER THREE

Two whole days off—an infrequent luxury—and the exhilaration of learning to windsurf, made Lissa feel refreshed and brimming with good spirits on Monday morning. She had acquired a smoother tan and her hair was a lighter shade of gold. For a change she plaited it, tucked the end under and tied a blue ribbon round it. She chose a blue tabard printed with monkeys swinging on trees to cover her uniform that day.

'Good weekend, by the look of you,' Karyn remarked as they were preparing a medications trolley. 'I wish I could tan as easily as you do.' She added, 'I hope you were lavish with the sunscreen. This is Australia, remember, top of the pops for skin cancer.'

'I was *very* lavish,' Lissa assured her. 'I went wind-surfing—it was fantastic! My favourite sport from now on!'

'Was Paul there?'

'Yes.' She emphasised, 'And a lot of other people.' She gave Karyn a sharp poke. 'Stop trying to pair me off with Paul, there's nothing doing.' She paused, her eye falling on the next prescription sheet. Something clicked in her mind. 'Hey, this isn't right. . .'

'What isn't?'

'Emily's medication.'

Karyn glanced at it. 'Yes, it is. That's what she's been having all along.'

'I know, but on Friday Hugo suggested it should be

40

changed as a precaution because there was a mild reaction. He discussed it with Jayne.'

'What was the alternative?'

'I don't know. I wasn't close enough to hear.'

'Well, perhaps he changed his mind and decided to stick with this one,' said Karyn. 'There's no new prescription.'

'Maybe I ought to check, just in case there's been a mix-up and it's got mislaid,' Lissa said worriedly.

'Well, Dr Rossney's with Warren at the moment,' said Karyn. 'You might as well ask her.'

Lissa went along to the charge nurse's office and knocked. Warren called, 'Come in!' Dr Rossney was still there. She glanced at Lissa as though resenting the interruption. 'Yes, Lissa?' said Warren.

'Sorry to interrupt,' Lissa apologised, 'but we're just doing the medications and I wanted to query Emily Grey's with Dr Rossney.'

A beautifully shaped eyebrow arched questioningly. 'Yes, what about her, Sister?'

'On Friday I thought Dr Stanfield suggested a change of antibiotic as Emily was showing reactions, but as there's no new prescription on the list I thought I'd better check.'

Jayne Rossney's lovely face changed from slightly amused indifference to a hardness of expression that made Lissa recoil. 'Her medication should have been changed,' the young doctor said. 'I distinctly remember giving the new prescription to you, Sister. Surely you remember?'

Lissa almost gasped. She had no such recollection.

'You were in charge, as I recall, because Warren was absent,' went on Jayne with a long-suffering glance at Warren. She gave Lissa a meaningful look. 'Perhaps you were so preoccupied with your plans for the weekend that you forgot.'

Lissa didn't know what to say. She glanced at Warren, who looked uncomfortable but not censorious. He said, 'Maybe Pharmacy. . .?'

Lissa, fuming, went back to Karyn. 'She swore black and blue she'd written the prescription,' she said. 'And I reckon she forgot, but she wasn't game to admit it to me or Warren.'

'Well, at least she admitted the change was agreed.'

'I get the feeling she doesn't like me,' Lissa said. 'I don't know what I've done to her.'

'You've just caught her out in a fairly serious omission,' pointed out Karyn. 'Doctors don't like being shown up by nurses.'

Lissa gritted her teeth. 'She's so damned superior. Just because she's a doctor she thinks no one else has got half a brain!' She flounced off and checked with Pharmacy with the negative result she expected, then reported back to Warren. Dr Rossney had gone.

'She did forget, didn't she?' said Lissa.

He didn't confirm it in so many words. 'All humans are fallible, Lissa.' She wasn't sure if he was referring to her or Jayne Rossney. Warren never took sides in arguments.

'Yes, I know.' Her anger was already cooling.

'And it's a fairly common human instinct to try and shift the blame for our mistakes on to others. Don't worry about it. You can be sure she will. She's very conscientious really.' He smiled, and she knew he had believed her, not the young doctor, when he said, 'Full marks for spotting the error.'

Lissa smiled, a little abashed. 'Sorry, but she gets my goat a bit. . . She looks down her nose at nurses.'

'She's young, newly qualified, and a bit insecure, so she covers up with superiority. She'll mellow.'

'You're the most fair-minded person I know,' said Lissa, feeling a little shamed. 'You ought to be a High Court judge.'

He laughed. 'I'd sure get better paid!'

The incident rankled with Lissa for an hour or two, but she was not one to brood over slights and soon forgot it. There was always too much to do on the children's ward to allow time for personal grievances to fester. Particularly as uppermost in her mind was her anxiety over the small boy called Toby.

Lissa was sure that he was a victim of abuse. She was also certain that she wasn't the only the one to think this; she already knew that Karyn was as suspicious as she was herself. Warren had been non-committal when she had broached the subject at a briefing, but the way his frown lines had deepened had convinced her that he also agreed. She wondered what, if anything, he had said to Hugo. What Paul thought she had not canvassed. They did not talk 'shop' when together, on his insistence, so there had not been an opportunity to broach the subject in an unofficial way. Mentioning her fears to Jayne Rossney was not something Lissa felt inclined to do. It was not up to her anyway; there was nothing she could do personally.

As Karyn had said only recently, 'You can't do anything except leave it to the powers that be, Lissa.'

Nevertheless, Lissa felt a surge of emotion every time she came near the little boy who was so quiet and withdrawn and, as she put it to Maggie during one of their rare evenings home together, so *resigned*.

'He accepts everything we do without a murmur,' she said sadly. 'Just looks at you with those big brown eyes like a trusting spaniel and hardly ever says a word. Please and thank you, yes and no, that's about all we ever get out of him. He has this scruffy little toy dog that he never lets go of, and if anyone tries to take it away that's the only time he shows any emotion. It's as though there's a person deep inside that tiny body, but it's hiding.'

'A lot of people are like that,' Maggie said. 'Hiding from something.'

Was Hugo? Lissa thought at once. That was exactly how she would describe Hugo too: as though the real man had shrunk back inside the shell, hiding from the world. But what could have made him do that? Maybe the rumours of divorce were true.

'If the child is a victim of abuse,' Maggie was saying, 'it's a problem for the social welfare people. There's nothing you can do about it, Lissa.'

Lissa clamped the lid on her thoughts about Hugo and slipped back into the conversation. 'I know. But he'll be going home in a few days, and I feel this awful dread. . .'

'Maybe you're being a little too imaginative,' suggested the always practical and down-to-earth Maggie.

Lissa clasped her hands behind her head and stared at the ceiling. 'Probably. I am a bit prone to flights of fancy, and wild surmises.' Like imagining that Hugo Stanfield had been compelled to seek her out because she had willed him to. At no time since he'd come in when she'd been feeding the baby had he sought her out or even cast a glance in her direction, despite the fact that she'd hovered.

Her encounters with Jayne Rossney had been cool since the incident of the prescription, and it was obvious to Lissa that Jayne avoided having her around when she was attending to patients. That there was actually a festering resentment she never dreamed, until one day Jayne came into the treatment room while Lissa and Leonie, one of the SENs, were sterilising feeding cups and bottles.

'Oh—Lissa. . .' The doctor's tone was crisp.

'Yes, Dr Rossney?' said Lissa formally.

'I've ordered a couple of changes to the feed formula for the anal fissure child and the intussusception that came back from theatre yesterday.' She gave a light laugh that contained no amusement. 'I thought I should warn you, just in case there's any problem. I wouldn't want there to be any more mistakes.'

Lissa seethed. The girl was emphasising the point because Leonie was there. Jayne Rossney knew perfectly well who had made the mistake. Leonie sensed an atmosphere and mumbling an excuse, hurried out of the room, while Lissa said. 'No, of course not. Thank you. I'll make sure there aren't.' She felt uncomfortable. The young doctor's dislike was almost palpable. Perhaps it had been a little tactless of her to ask her about that prescription in front of Warren, and she was sorry she had done so now, if it had caused antipathy between her and Jayne. But no way was she going to apologise.

Dr Rossney turned at the door. 'I'm sure you will,' she said with heavily sarcastic emphasis which made Lissa's lips part in surprise. 'You're so efficient, aren't you, Sister? Just because you were trained in a big London hospital, you think you know it all. Well, you don't. It might pay you to remember you're only a nurse, or one of these days you'll step out of line and find yourself in deep trouble.'

Lissa was thunderstruck at this tirade. 'Dr Rossney, I don't think. . .'

'Oh, you're all sweetness and light, aren't you, especially with the male medicos, and you'd never resist an opportunity to downgrade another female to them, would you? I suppose you're the typical doctor-hero-worshipping nurse one reads about in novels.'

'What have I ever done to you?' Lissa asked, aghast.

Jayne's face had reddened and she seemed aware that she had let her tongue run away with her. 'Tittle-tattling to Dr Stanfield isn't very ethical,' she said, her tone modified, but still resentful. 'I suppose you hoped to ingratiate yourself by telling him about that minor prescription mix-up?'

Lissa, outraged, took a step towards her. '*I* didn't tell him! Frankly, Dr Rossney, I resent the accusation—especially as you falsely accused me! I've got better things to do than tell tales on junior doctors!'

Her last words carried an implied insult that she did not intend, but which the young doctor obviously read into them. Jayne tossed her dark hair and her eyes flashed, but with uncertainty now.

'If anyone told Dr Stanfield,' Lissa said evenly, 'it must have been Warren. Which he had a perfect right to do, in the interests of the patients. Why don't you go and tear a strip off him?' Had Hugo torn a strip off Jayne as a result of it? Lissa wondered, uncharitably thinking that it served her right. And was that why she felt bound to take out her resentment on someone? No wonder she'd been treating Lissa like a pariah lately!

The eyes of the two women met, each flashing sparks. Then Jayne tossed her head again and, flinging open the door, departed, but not before she'd said cuttingly, 'You might fancy Hugo, Sister, but I can assure you he definitely does not fancy you!' And the triumphant look she shot at Lissa clearly stated that if anyone were the object of his fancying, it was her.

The door closed sharply and Lissa found she was trembling. What an encounter! What a rude, self-opinionated, arrogant. . .she stopped and quietly laughed to herself. There was no point in getting uptight about it. Unwittingly, she'd made an enemy of Jayne Rossney, and even though the doctor's accusation was unfounded, that wasn't going to change anything. What dismayed Lissa more was that Jayne might have recognised that her regard for Hugo was more than professional respect. Or was it simply that, in love with the man herself, Jayne regarded all other females in his orbit as rivals? As she did herself, Lissa admitted, although she would never have attacked anyone with so much venom. After all, Jayne's chances were at least fifty-fifty; her own were zero.

Lissa was more shaken by the encounter with Jayne than she cared to admit. She had never had such a confrontation before in her life, and the unfairness of it rankled. On reflection, she thought perhaps she shouldn't have been quite so forceful to someone who was, after all, a superior, but she had been taken by surprise, with no time to consider their relative positions in the hospital. They had just been two women flaring up at each other. I must not be so volatile, Lissa cautioned herself. Maybe that came from being the middle one in the family and needing to stick up for herself more.

When Toby went home, Lissa watched with misgivings as his mother took him away. Tears of anger and

frustration filled her eyes, and deep inside her was fear
for the little boy she had come to love so much.

'I wonder how long it'll be before we see that little
darling again.' It was Vi Downing talking beside her,
and sounding just as choked. She was a middle-aged
woman who had come back to nursing now her children
were old enough to fend for themselves.

Lissa glanced at her. 'It's awful, isn't it?'

'He's a real poppet, that one. I reckon he'd be
talking if he weren't so cowed. He's not retarded, I'm
sure of that. I got him to join in a nursery rhyme the
other day, and there was this little tiny whisper of a
voice as though he was afraid to make a noise.' She
paused and swallowed hard. 'Hey, we're not supposed
to get involved, Lissa!'

'I know. . .but it's hard, Vi. Some of them just
wrench your heartstrings.'

Vi forced a laugh. 'Until you have a brood of your
own. Then you know what it's all about. Many a time
I've wanted to wallop my lot.'

'But not *hurt* them. Not deliberately.'

'No, of course not,' Vi said seriously, 'but there is a
fine line, Lissa, and some people don't have the control
others have. A social worker has been to see the
family, did you know that?'

'Yes. I just hope the counselling works, that's all.'

'They have to be careful when there's no proof. And
it's very hard to prove anything.'

'I know.'

Toby was so much on her mind that day that Lissa
eventually couldn't help unburdening herself to Warren
when she was in his office helping to tidy up some case
notes of discharged patients.

'I know how you feel,' he said in his quiet, un-emotional way. 'I've got kids myself. It's beyond comprehension that a parent could ill-treat a child, especially one not much more than a baby.'

'They should be taken away. . .the parents jailed,' Lissa said emphatically.

Warren shook his head. 'I know that seems logical, but it isn't always the best thing for the child. We're in a special position, Lissa, because we see what others don't and recognise what might elude teachers and friends and relatives, but we're not here to make judgements. All we can do is inform the appropriate authorities of our suspicions, and at the same time give support to the parents while also giving protection to the child.'

'That's a tall order!'

'I agree. But you must keep a balance in these cases. Child abuse is more complex than most of us realise. Sometimes it's only the result of a momentary loss of temper, and is deeply regretted. Too drastic a reaction could lead to family breakdown and a host of other evils that wouldn't benefit the child. We have to leave the decisions to the psychologists, Lissa.'

'Toby suffers psychological abuse, I'm certain. That's why he isn't talking yet.'

'Vi told me about the nursery rhyme and how he whispered it. Don't worry, Lissa, everything has been noted and reported. A social worker will be keeping an eye on the Foremans now Toby's gone home.'

'I guess I don't understand too well,' acknowledged Lissa, 'and I've not had any children of my own, but I've got brothers and sisters, and we all grew up in a happy loving family. It's hard to imagine any other kind. That's why I get so angry, I suppose.'

Warren smiled. 'And why you're the right kind of person for nursing, Lissa. Have you thought about applying for a charge nurse position?'

She looked at him in surprise. 'No, I hadn't. I haven't been back long, anyway.'

'You were here for two years before. That counts.'

She glanced sharply at him. 'Are you leaving?'

He nodded. 'Keep it under your hat. I'm just about certain I've got a Matron's job at a private hospital in my suburb. I think it'll suit me very well.'

Lissa was stunned. 'Well, congratulations!'

'Don't jump the gun! I'm not saying anything here yet. But if you're interested, you could probably have this job. I'd give you the recommendation. You're the senior nurse on this ward, you've got your ped. certificate, and the experience.' He smiled. 'The only snag is the paperwork!'

'I'm flattered,' said Lissa. 'I suppose I would like it. . . I just hadn't thought about promotion. I do tend to drift along if I'm happy in what I'm doing. I'm not particularly ambitious.'

'More anxious to get married and have a family?'

'One day, maybe.' When she could look at a man and not see Hugo's face, she thought gloomily. Which might be never.

'Well, meanwhile, do you want me to put you forward if the occasion arises?'

'Yes, please,' she decided. 'And thanks. I appreciate your confidence in me.'

'Just don't go running off back to the UK again too soon,' he admonished with a smile.

The day I hear that Hugo Stanfield is going to marry Jayne Rossney, I might have no alternative, Lissa thought, as she went back on the ward later. I couldn't stand working with them if that happened. Oh, why can't he fall in love with me, not her! In spite of herself, the chant was back in her mind, insidiously invading her subconscious. Love me, not her, love me, not her.

'Fool!' she derided herself. 'Wicked witch!'

Lissa didn't realise she had spoken aloud until the child she was trying to interest in a jigsaw puzzle looked at her and said, perfectly seriously, 'Are you a witch, Lissa?'

Lissa gulped. 'No, of course not!' Heavens, she'd be in hot water for scaring the patients if she wasn't careful.

'Oh,' said Tania, aged six. 'I wish you were a witch. I like witches.'

'Well, sometimes I pretend,' said Lissa to satisfy her. 'But I only make good spells, like in ten minutes Tania Brown will have finished her jigsaw.' She waved her hands in front of the child's face. 'Abracadabra, Tania Brown. You are very smart. You can finish your jigsaw in ten minutes.'

Whether it was good or bad psychology, Lissa wasn't sure, but Tania, who was difficult to hold to any activity for more than five minutes, suddenly turned her whole attention to the jigsaw and started matching the pieces, her pale elfin face rigid with concentration. She was recovering from a kidney operation and would be going home soon. With luck she would survive on her remaining kidney and never need a transplant.

There were only a few pieces left and Tania was excitedly trying them this way and that when her mother arrived, breathless and apologising for being later than usual.

'Hi, Mum,' said Tania. 'Lissa's a witch.'

'Is she really?' Tania's mother was an actress with a

lilting voice that carried. 'A real witch? Well, imagine!' A peal of indulgent laughter echoed around the ward.

'She put a spell on me to make me smart so I could finish the jigsaw in ten minutes.'

Tania's mother took this in her stride. 'Well, aren't you a lucky little girl! I wish she'd put a spell on me to help me learn my lines.' She didn't seem to require any explanation, so Lissa didn't bother to invent one. But she'd better be careful about speaking her thoughts aloud in future, she thought. It was a bad failing of hers.

Lissa left the mother and daughter together and immediately ran into Paul, who had evidently heard Althea Brown's remark.

'What all this about being a witch?' he joked. 'Where's your broomstick and black cat?'

'Only after midnight,' she returned gaily.

'Can I come up and see your stovepipe hat some time?' he growled in a mock sexy tone.

'Only genuine wizards are invited,' she shot back.

He rolled his eyes lasciviously, 'I'm a real wizard at. . .'

'That's enough, Dr Norris—I'm busy,' said Lissa. She hoped none of the other nurses had heard Mrs Brown's remarks. Being teased about being a witch was a bit too close to the bone. She still had guilt feelings. 'Do you have a patient to see?'

'We've just admitted a multiple fracture. Fell off a roof. Arms, legs and collarbone. He was lucky he didn't break his neck.'

'Oh, that's awful! He'll be in traction for months. How old?'

'Twelve. Ought to have had more sense,' said Paul.

'Bit of a tearaway, according to his mother. Daredevil. I suggested if he wants to scale roofs in future, he should take up hang-gliding.'

'Now that's something I'd really like to do, but it's a bit scary,' Lissa said, her eyes lighting up.

'I thought you were hooked on windsurfing now.'

'I am, but I think hang-gliding would be great. I wouldn't mind going scuba-diving too.'

He flung an arm around her shoulders and would not let her jerk it away as they walked to the door. 'Why don't you take up something romantic and feminine for a change, like embroidery or knitting?'

Lissa laughed. 'I might get clucky, and then you'd be scared to go out with me.'

'I might change my mind.'

Paul's expression was not serious, but his face was very close. The doorway was screened by partitions so they were out of sight of the patients, and Lissa knew he was going to give her a quick kiss. She dodged, but the move only served to make him jerk her close and their noses almost collided. At the same moment the door opened and Hugo walked in, followed by Jayne Rossney. Hugo looked them both up and down with an expression bordering on disgust, and Jayne smirked.

'Well, this is a cosy corner, isn't it? Are we interrupting?' she asked sweetly.

'Sister Moran tripped and I was helping her up,' said Paul blandly, and Lissa cursed him. It was such a transparent excuse. She knew her face was scarlet, so she muttered something unintelligible and fled. To be caught twice with Paul in compromising circumstances was the worst kind of luck. Well, she thought grimly, there wasn't going to be a third time. Jayne Rossney wasn't going to smirk at *her* like that again. She was going to have to take Paul to task.

That evening, Maggie said, 'Well, I wouldn't be too hard on him. After all, it might just have made your Dr Stanfield jealous.'

'That's a joke! Why should he be, and why should I care anyway? He's not *my* Dr Stanfield.'

Maggie laughed. 'Come on, Lissa, I wasn't born yesterday. You're a bit keen on Hugo Stanfield, admit it.'

'I don't know what makes you think. . .' Lissa could feel her colour giving her away.

'You're always talking about him, what he said, what he did.'

Lissa was astonished. 'I am?'

'Well, it's not the walls talking.' Maggie lifted the nail varnish brush she was wielding and poked it towards Lissa. 'Are you in love with him? Is that why you came back?'

Lissa's defences were down. Tears suddenly welled up. 'Yes.' She buried her face in her hands. 'It's stupid, Maggie, absolutely crazy. He's not in the least interested in me, never will be. There's this glamorous young intern who obviously adores him. . .'

'Maybe he doesn't realise *you* do,' Maggie suggested. 'Poor old Henry says he thought I hated the sight of him! Imagine! I was practically grovelling at his feet and he didn't recognise the signs. Men are thick sometimes. Maybe you should give Hugo a little clue now and then.'

'I don't even see him very often, and he avoids me anyhow. I did think for a while he was showing interest, but I was wrong, Maggie. It was wishful thinking, that's all.'

'Well, if he saw you canoodling with Paul, he might well steer clear. He might not be the type to poach on another's territory. You'll have to let him know where you stand with Paul.'

'I've already done that,' Lissa said miserably, 'but he believes his eyes, not his ears. Look, let's not talk about it. I feel a fool—really ashamed of myself, getting a crush on a doctor. That's adolescent stuff.'

'At your age,' said Maggie, dipping the brush deep into scarlet varnish, 'it's more likely to be love. Don't give up. Stranger things have happened. Who knows, there might be a moment when your stars collide, and whoopee, there you are, in his arms, and he'll be promising love forever.'

'You're taking the mickey,' Lissa said sourly. 'I'm going to make a cup of coffee. I'll bring you one if you promise not to mention Hugo again.'

Maggie grinned. 'I won't be the one who mentions him!'

Lissa threw a cushion at her friend's head. 'I hope your nail varnish all peels off!' she yelled, dodging the returned cushion as she went out.

The next day was hectic. There were more young patients being discharged and admitted than usual. Lissa found herself having to help with the bedmaking, as well as her other chores. There seemed to be parents all over the place, and even children with the sunniest natures seemed to be in crotchety moods. Lissa was run off her feet trying to soothe and placate, while not letting her patience reach the end of its tether.

Vi Downing said once, handing her a screaming baby, 'I know I'm a mother, but you've got the magic touch, Lissa. See what you can do with this little mite.

I've tried everything. Dr Norris said she's not to have another sedative yet.'

It was Annabel, who was recovering from a bad scalding to her legs which had required skin grafts. Clearly there was still considerable discomfort, if not actual pain.

Lissa took the screaming child in her arms. 'What's the matter, darling?' She rocked the baby gently against her shoulder, crooning softly to her. 'Are your poor legs hurting? Let me have a look.'

Her soothing voice continued as she carried the child into the treatment-room and laid her on the examination table. She unwound the light bandages that protected the grafts from being scratched. They were a little too tight, she thought. The child's legs were still a bit puffy. As soon as the pressure was relieved, Annabel's screams stopped, but she continued sobbing. Lissa comforted her, swabbed the almost healed tissue with a cooling anti-irritant and replaced the coverings more loosely but so that they would not too easily come adrift. She was rewarded with a sudden bright smile. The two feverish spots on the baby's cheeks began to fade.

'That's better! Now let's wipe those tears away.' She dabbed Annabel's face with a damp flannel, and tickled her under the ribs. 'Let's see you giggle.'

Happier now, Annabel obliged. After a few moments of teasing play, Lissa picked the child up and settled her on the crook of her arm. 'Now we'll go and find Teddy.'

Suddenly sensing that she was not alone, Lissa glanced over her shoulder and her heart flipped at the sight of Hugo Stanfield framed in the treatment-room doorway. He strolled in, and Lissa had the oddest feeling, as she had had once before, that he had no good reason to be there, but somehow couldn't help himself. And as before, to her mind, he even looked a trifle puzzled, as though he'd caught himself sleepwalking.

'You seem to have restored Annabel's sunny disposition,' he remarked. If he'd heard her screaming he must have been watching almost since she had come in.

'Yes, she's all right now. She was itching, that's all, and very uncomfortable.'

'Bandages too tight, I suppose.'

Lissa nodded.

'Not your doing?'

'No.' Lissa was not about to tell him who had done the last dressing. She would have a quiet word to the new SEN, Leonie, herself.

Annabel suddenly held out her arms to Hugo. 'Da-da!' she gurgled delightedly, struggling to leave Lissa.

Lissa raised an eyebrow and grinned. 'How many times have you been called "Da-da" today?' He was ignoring the baby's attentions, and when Lissa held Annabel towards him it suddenly occurred to her that she had never actually seen him spontaneously pick up a child. She'd never seen him hold a baby in his arms for other than purely medical reasons. She was curious to see how he handled this one.

'Go on, give her a cuddle,' she said boldly. 'All little girls miss their daddies, and this one's is overseas at the moment, isn't he, love? He's an airline pilot.' Annabel was reaching eagerly for Hugo, so Lissa pushed her closer. 'Come on, you're supposed to like children!'

Hugo's arms seemed to come up reluctantly, but he

took the little girl into them, ruffled her fine fair hair and mumbled baby-talk as though he was nervous. But what startled Lissa was the flash of panic she'd seen in his eyes, almost as though he was afraid to hold the child. She was too close to be mistaken. But she was puzzled. Why would a man who dealt with children every day of his life medically be afraid to take one in his arms in a casual way? Was the highly respected paediatrician no more than that after all, a man with no personal feelings, who saw children as patients to be healed, who could switch on a bedside manner when required, but who took no personal pleasure from being with children? The discovery shocked her. She felt her admiration begin to crumble, her love to waver.

She said, 'Were you looking for Warren?'

He looked at her as though she'd said something bizarre, then said, 'Warren—yes. Yes, I was looking for Warren.'

'He's probably at lunch.'

'Well, I'll come back later.' He thrust Annabel back at Lissa. It was almost as though he were passing a hot cake, glad to relinquish her. For a moment his eyes flicked quickly from Lissa's face to the child's, lingering on Annabel's with an expression that defied interpretation. Lissa was beginning to feel an irrational kind of anger with him. She didn't want him to be the kind of man she all at once suspected he was. She didn't want him to be cold and clinical, his attitude purely an acquired professional façade.

'Don't you think she's pretty?' she said, smoothing the fair curls. 'Her daddy dotes on her, so her mother says. He's very upset that she hurt herself and he's rushing back as quick as he can to see her. Isn't she a lucky little girl?' Annabel smiled as smugly as though she was aware of her power over her parents.

'It's a pity the doting doesn't run to looking after them properly,' Hugo said in a tone that made Lissa's gaze snap sharply back to him. 'A child that age scalded as badly as she was! The scars will never completely disappear, you know.'

'You're not blaming the parents, are you?' Lissa was shocked. 'Accidents do happen.'

'Most accidents are preventable. If people took more care to make their homes safe for small children, our beds wouldn't be so full all the time.'

Although there was truth in what he said, Lissa was taken aback at his unexpectedly judgemental tone. 'You're obviously not a parent! It isn't possible to keep an eye on a small child every minute of the day, especially if you have other children.' She added scathingly, 'You'll be telling me next you still believe that cot deaths could be prevented if parents were more vigilant.'

His face darkened with fury, and Lissa wished she hadn't let him goad her into making that last remark. Parental neglect was never a factor in a cot death. That had been proved over and over, nevertheless she had often had to reassure parents that they had no need to feel guilty. She attempted to make amends. 'Parents do feel guilty whatever happens to their child,' she said. 'As you're not a parent, perhaps you don't understand the anguish they go through. Being a paediatrician isn't the same as being a father.'

The air between them crackled as he looked at her for a moment, searingly, and she wondered why she was feeling quite so outraged, why she had let him rub her up the wrong way when there was no real cause.

Lissa expected an angry retort and a rebuke for her temerity in speaking so insultingly to him. When he said nothing, she opened her mouth to apologise, but before she could say a word he tore his eyes from her face and strode out of the room, slamming the door behind him.

CHAPTER FOUR

LISSA deeply regretted the incident with Hugo. The fact that minor irritation had briefly flared between them on other occasions was no consolation. Before, it had only been trivial. Today she had gone too far. What had got into her, she didn't know. What she did know was that Hugo had been extremely angry when he had stalked out of the treatment-room. She had insulted him, and that was unforgivable. It would serve her right if he had her removed from the ward forthwith.

Which mightn't be a bad thing, she reflected, even while feeling the agony of loss as acutely as if it had already happened; then maybe she would forget about him. She knew that wasn't likely. If she hadn't been able to do it twelve thousand miles away, then a few corridors or flights of stairs between them were hardly likely to effect a cure. In spite of her despair, she smiled wryly at a bizarre image of Dr Stanfield being compelled by her wayward subconscious—or witchcraft—to keep visiting Geriatrics or Women's Medical or wherever she was banished to, and having to explain himself without knowing how he came to be there. But it wasn't really funny, it was mortifying. Tragic.

Later that day, Warren noticed her gloom and remarked on it. 'What's up, Lissa? You look like someone who's been forced to eat pink blancmange!'

In spite of herself, Lissa was forced to laugh. Her aversion to the bright pink dessert that frequently appeared on the meal trolleys was a standing joke, especially since the day one child had thrown his at the wallpaper, to be instantly emulated by several enthusiastic copycats before she could stop them.

'Actually, it ought to be humble pie,' she said on an overwhelming urge to confess. 'I was rude to Hugo.'

Warren's eyebrows rose. 'That's not like you. Why?'

'I don't know. . .' She wished she hadn't started to tell him. If Warren guessed. . . She went on quickly, 'He bugs me a bit. I don't know where I am with him, somehow. One minute he's friendly, the next brusque. You can't—well, get through to him.' She realised she was admitting that she would like to.

He eyed her closely. 'What did you say to him?'

She couldn't get out of telling him now. 'I didn't mean to be offensive, but we were talking about accidents to children in the home and he said most of them could be prevented. I know he's right, but for some reason I acted perversely. I twitted him about not understanding what it's like to be a parent since he isn't one himself, and I said I supposed he was one of the old school who still thought parents were to blame for cot deaths too.'

Warren whistled low. 'Hell!'

Lissa was startled at his vehement reaction. 'It was a stupid thing to say, and I didn't mean it. I know he doesn't really think that, but my tongue ran away with me. He makes me feel argumentative sometimes.' She added defensively, 'I think it was his attitude to Annabel. She wanted to go to him, but he didn't seem to want to hold her because there was no medical reason for it, and when he did, he shoved her back at me almost straight away as though she was contaminated. He suddenly seemed so—unfeeling, I suppose. . .' She trailed away. She wasn't making very good sense.

Warren studied her thoughtfully for a moment or two, then said, 'Come into my office.'

Lissa followed meekly. Now I've done it, she thought. He'll read me the riot act, how not to behave towards consultant paediatricians, and he's very sorry but in the circumstances he can't put me forward for promotion. I've blown it. Why didn't I just stick it out in London and cure myself there? It would have happened in time. It serves me right for being so impetuous. . .

'Sit down, Lissa,' said Warren, interrupting her thoughts.

Wearily, she sat. He didn't take the chair behind his desk, but perched on the edge of the desk near her, arms folded across his chest and a more sympathetic expression on his face than she deserved. Lissa felt very small and ashamed. Then Warren said, 'You ought to think before you speak, Lissa, but I know that's sometimes hard, especially when you're pressured, and, let's face it, we're all under pressure here.'

'That's not an excuse,' she said, then tentatively, 'Should I go and apologise to him?'

He considered her for a moment. She looked so contrite, and forlorn. The trouble with Lissa was that under a happy-go-lucky exterior she was deeply emotional, with a strong conscience. Warren was anxious to help her, and Hugo too, so he said, 'You'll have to make up your own mind about that after what I'm going to tell you. You see, you didn't just insult Hugo, my dear, you undoubtedly wounded him deeply.'

'Wounded him? How?' Lissa broke in, perplexed.

'You couldn't know, so I'm going to tell you something in confidence that you must never let go any further.'

Lissa straightened in surprise. 'About Hugo?' Her stomach was tightening in an ominous way.

Warren's face was grave. 'Yes. What most people at SCG don't know and what Hugo evidently prefers them not to know is that a few years ago his baby daughter was a SIDS victim.'

Lissa felt her face lose all colour as she stared at him in horror. 'Oh, no!' She covered her face with her hands, then looked up at him, stricken. 'Oh, Warren. . .and I said. . .'

'Only a year later, his wife was killed in a car accident. He doesn't know I know this. He didn't tell me; I happen to know because his parents and mine are slightly acquainted. They all live in Perth and play bowls at the same club. Last Christmas Hugo happened to come up in conversation when I was home for the holidays—Mrs Stanfield had apparently been expressing concern about him to my mother.'

Lissa was sunk in deep remorse. To have, even unwittingly, reopened so deep a wound was unforgivable. To have thought him cold and unfeeling, to have felt angry with him because she believed he was only a good doctor, not a warm person, was the most terrible error of her whole life. For a few moments she could not speak, she was so shattered. At last she said slowly, 'That must be why he avoids showing his feelings with the children. I'd noticed a kind of reserve sometimes, but he's so good with them it's well covered most of the time. It didn't strike me forcefully until he seemed to deliberately reject Annabel. But now I understand why he was reluctant to cuddle her just for the pleasure of it—she reminded him. . .oh, Warren, what am I going to do? Won't it make it worse if I say I'm sorry? But how am I going to face him if I don't?'

He looked at her steadily. 'You'll have to make that decision yourself, Lissa. If you do decide an apology is called for, I think you should tell Hugo what you know, and how you came to find out.' He paused, his expression demanding. 'Promise me you won't breathe a word of this to anyone else?'

'I wouldn't dream of gossiping about him, Warren.' Lissa rose unsteadily. 'Thanks for telling me.' After a long pause, she added in a low tone, 'Do you think I should transfer to another ward?'

Warren considered the proposal. 'No, I don't.' He smiled reassuringly. 'Just remember that everyone has their vulnerable spots. Maybe Hugo still licks his wounds too much. He needs to start living in the world again.' He paused, then said in all seriousness, 'Maybe you can help him to do that.'

'Me? After what I said to him? He'll never speak to me again except when he has to.'

'That depends,' said Warren.

'On what?'

'On how you handle this.'

'I don't think I trust myself to handle anything after this. Warren, what can I say to him?' she pleaded desperately.

'You'll think of something,' he said, not unkindly. 'I can't help you any more, Lissa, but I will say this: I personally think Hugo needs to be shaken out of his remorse and guilt. It's destroying him.'

'I can understand why he's so dedicated to research into SIDS,' Lissa said. 'I don't mean it isn't because he cares about other people's grief, because I've always thought he does, deeply—well, until today, when I suddenly doubted him—but he must also need to know the answers for his own peace of mind.' She bunched the material of the pale primrose cover-up she was wearing with clenching fingers. 'How could I have thought, even for a minute, that he was unfeeling. . .?'

'Don't blame yourself too much, Lissa. You couldn't have known. You made your judgements on the evidence before you.'

'I hope I shall never do that again. Things are so often not what they seem.'

Sounds of activity drifted through from the corridor, voices, a burst of laughter, hurrying feet. The next shift was coming on. Warren glanced at his watch. 'You're off now?'

'Yes. I've just got a couple of things to do before I hand over, and some notes to write up.'

Lissa went home with a heavy heart. She was still stinging with embarrassment and shame. How was she going to face Hugo tomorrow? Could she bring herself to go to his office, ask to see him and apologise? And could she apologise without telling him what she knew? Yet, if she told him, wouldn't that make it all much worse? She would be adding injury to insult, opening the wounds even more. Maybe she should just let it ride and be more careful in future.

She was glad that Maggie wasn't home; she might have poured it all out to her flatmate if she had been. She knew Maggie would advise apologising. Warren had obliquely sanctioned that course too, Lissa reminded herself.

She paced the living-room of the flat endlessly, drinking coffee and wishing she had the courage to do what she ought to do. But knowing what she should do and doing it were two different things. It was going to be so difficult to face him. She was sure she would burst into tears, or her words would come out all wrong. She might even make it much worse. If only she didn't have to wait until tomorrow, if only she could get it over with now!

Suddenly the solution occurred to her. Why not phone him? She put down her coffee mug and reached for the L–Z phone book. There were not many Stanfields, and only four with the initial H. He lived not far away, she recalled. Rosewood Avenue, hadn't he said? There was no Stanfield, with or without the initial H, in the book in her suburb. Of course, he isn't here, she thought, this is the old book. He hasn't been in Melbourne long enough to be in it.

She tried Directory Enquiries. Yes, there was a Dr Hugo Stanfield living in Armadale, but his was an ex-directory number. Lissa put the phone down with a sigh. She almost picked it up again to ring the hospital, who would have the number, then changed her mind. They mightn't give it to her without good reason, and what reason could she give for wanting to ring him tonight? There was bound to be speculation unless she had a very good one. It was better not to risk gossip. She hunched herself on the chair by the phone, defeated.

But, more than ever now, she felt compelled to make reparation right away for what she had done. She wanted to talk to him tonight before her courage evaporated. She knew she wouldn't be able to sleep with this hanging over her. Rosewood Avenue was perhaps ten minutes' walk from her flat. But she didn't know what number he lived at. She could ask, she thought. Someone was bound to know. Or she might be lucky and see his car parked in the driveway. Of course he might not be home, or in a hurry to go out.

'Oh, stop looking for excuses,' she finally told herself. 'Go round there and see. If you can't see him, you can't, and that's all there is to it. You'll have to wait until tomorrow.'

Lissa showered and changed into white cotton trousers and a cool strawberry-pink top. She fastened her hair at the nape with a pink flowered clasp. It was nearly seven when she finally set off, and walked briskly in the direction of Rosewood Avenue. It was still hot, and she felt flushed and sticky when she reached the shady tree-lined street. There were large houses along both sides, with one or two blocks of apartments between them. Lissa strolled along one side looking for Hugo's car, but most driveways were empty. There were lock-up garages at almost every house, as she ought to have realised there would be in this upmarket area of the suburb.

Inspection of the other side proved just as fruitless, so she decided to ask someone. At the first house she tried there was no one home. As she walked back down the garden path, a car drew into the driveway next door and a man got out. It wasn't Hugo. When she asked if he knew where Dr Stanfield lived, he looked at her suspiciously for a moment, but she had come prepared and showed him her security tag. 'I'm a nurse at the hospital and I—I have something to deliver to him, but I've lost the address. . .' She saw with relief that the man was convinced.

'Number twenty-two,' he said. 'Just along on the right.'

Lissa thanked him and, heart hammering now, she

retraced her steps to number twenty-two. It was an Edwardian villa with verandas and creeper-covered walls. The brick driveway was comparatively new, but the red and ochre tiles patterning the veranda floor were originals. She paused for a moment, heart in her mouth, throat dry as dust, then reminded herself that she hadn't walked all this way in the heat to be a coward. She pushed the bell.

Lissa tried not to hope he wasn't home. This had to be got over with. She would know no peace until she had made hers with Hugo. The door opened suddenly and a middle-aged woman looked questioningly at her. His housekeeper, Lissa guessed.

'Good evening. . .' Lissa faltered. 'Is Dr Stanfield in?'

'He's just going out,' the woman said. 'If it's a GP you're looking for. . .'

'No, I'm a nurse from the hospital. I—er—need to see him rather urgently. I won't keep him long.'

The woman regarded her even more suspiciously than the neighbour. 'What's your name?'

Lissa told her. He might refuse to see me, she thought in panic. He might say he hasn't got time.

'Just a minute,' said the housekeeper, and half closed the door.

When it opened again, Hugo stood there looking down at Lissa in astonishment. 'Come in.' He looked neither pleased nor displeased.

'I—I'm sorry to disturb you,' Lissa said, stepping over the highly polished step into the hall. 'I know you're going out, but if you can spare five minutes. . .' She was floundering badly, and heaven knew how she was going to get the point of her visit.

'I was going out,' he said, as though her coming had caused him to abandon it.

'I won't keep you long,' she said. At least he didn't look angry now. He seemed more bemused by her unexpected appearance.

He ushered her into the living-room, which she could not help looking around admiringly. It was expensively and comfortably furnished, and there was a patch of evening sunshine on the thick-piled carpet near the french windows which gave the room a mellow atmosphere.

'Sit down, Lissa,' said Hugo, indicating an armchair. 'Would you like a drink? Short or long? I presume you walked here, so perhaps a long thirst-quencher?'

'Thank you. Anything, really. Well, yes, I am a bit thirsty. It's still hot outside. Lovely and cool in here, though. These old houses are wonderful for keeping the heat out, aren't they?' She stopped. She must not prattle. She must not lose sight of her reason for being there. Not that he was likely to let her do that. Perhaps he'd already guessed.

He went out to fetch some ice, then handed her a tall frosted glass, saying, 'It's mostly orange juice.' He poured himself a whisky, added ice and a squirt of soda and then sat opposite her. 'Cheers.'

Lissa lifted her glass, but said nothing. A heavy silence in the room brought the sound of a car into prominence, a bird call, a child's shrill squeal. Lissa felt tongue-tied. But it was up to her to state her business. He was waiting.

She sipped her drink and then put it on the side table near her. Hands tightly entwined in her lap, she blurted out, 'I came to apologise, Hugo. I'm truly sorry for saying what I did today. It was rude and insulting and

I didn't really mean it, I just. . .' She ran down, then took a deep breath and in the face of his impassive reception of her words, went on, 'Well, I don't know what came over me. If I'd had any idea. . .' Again she trailed off, disconcerted by his dark penetrating gaze. He had placed his own drink on the lamp table beside him and was looking at her intently over touching fingertips.

'Any idea of what?' he prompted in a low voice. His dark eyebrows angled to the bridge of his straight nose, and his mouth was set in an uncompromising line.

'Of—of your background,' she muttered. 'I'm so sorry, Hugo. I didn't know. I wouldn't have hurt you for worlds. . .' She leaned forward, distraught. 'I know I shouldn't have said what I did anyway, but that makes it so much worse. . .'

'What do you know, and who told you?' he rapped out.

Lissa flinched, but had to tell him. 'I was upset because I knew I'd offended you, and I told Warren. I asked him if he thought I should apologise and he said that was up to me, but that I ought to know something first. His parents apparently know yours and he found out about your—your wife and baby at Christmas.' She saw him flinch and added quickly, 'I'm quite sure he hasn't told anyone else. He respects your privacy.'

'What about you?' His upper lip curled a little. 'It's a nice bit of gossip to entertain your colleagues with in the nurses' room, isn't it?'

Lissa felt anger rising, but controlled it. She wasn't going to row with him, not even let him rile her. 'Do you really think I'm like that?' she asked quietly.

Hugo rose from his chair, taking his drink, and walked to the windows. His shoulders were a stiff line in the pearl grey suit, his back rigid. If he was having some difficulty in controlling his emotions, he concealed it well. After what seemed an interminable time, he turned round. His face was composed, but the deepened frown lines, the rigidity in his jaw and the slight twitching at the corner of his mouth betrayed inner conflict.

'I'm sorry I woke it all up again for you,' Lissa said softly. 'I know some things are very hard to forget.' A long silence followed her words. She stood up. 'I'd better go now.'

He took a step towards her. 'You haven't finished your drink.'

'No. But wouldn't you rather. . .?' Her hands were trembling so much that she shoved them into the pockets of her trousers. She had an almost overwhelming desire to throw her arms around him and comfort him, but she knew that sort of demonstration would be misunderstood and unwelcome. She recognised, looking at him now, that love had many more dimensions than she had imagined. It wasn't pity she felt for him, but a deep compassion and a yearning to help. It was tearing her apart inside knowing how he had suffered and still did, and that she had unwittingly added to his suffering.

'No, stay and finish your drink. Sit down, Lissa. I want to talk to you.' Lissa obeyed and reached for her drink. As she sipped the sharp cool liquid, he went on, 'I said I was going out, and I was. To see you.'

'To see me?' She was so astounded she almost spilled her drink. 'But why?'

He rolled his glass between his two hands. 'I wanted to explain my odd behaviour. You caught me on the raw and I overreacted. I didn't want you to think I was angry with you. I thought I ought to explain why I'd seemed so. . .so reluctant to make a fuss of Annabel. I couldn't explain right then because I was too churned up.'

'I suppose any little girl reminds you of your daughter,' Lissa ventured.

He looked at her blankly for a moment, then took a long swig of whisky. 'Annabel more than most. She's so like her it's uncanny. Natasha was blonde and blue-eyed with a little turned-up nose too. Even the way she smiles is the same. Holding her was like holding Natasha, her little hand clasping my finger. It all came back, everything. . .the whole damn nightmare. You see, it's exactly five years today since my daughter died.'

Lissa felt the tears welling up in her eyes and running down her cheeks. 'Oh, Hugo, I'm so sorry,' she whispered. 'If only I'd known. . .' She choked back a sob. 'Please, don't talk about it. . . Warren told me all I need to know. Don't torture yourself.'

'There's not a lot to tell,' he said in a level but emotionally charged voice. 'You might as well hear it from my side. Natasha died just as every other SIDS baby dies, suddenly, without warning, no significant symptoms. Angie, my wife, put her to bed as usual. In the morning she was dead. She was just ten months old. Of course we blamed ourselves, we blamed each other, we reacted the way all parents react on the death of a child. Angie was grief-stricken, and so was I—our first child. Gone. It just didn't seem possible. We were both doctors, both paediatricians. It couldn't happen to us. The guilt, the recriminations, were worse because of that. It drove us apart in the end. When Angie was killed by a drunken Saturday night driver, we hadn't been living together for nearly a year. Yet I felt guilty about that too, as though somehow it was all my fault. The driver of the other car went to prison for dangerous driving, but I still felt responsible. I felt that somehow *I* should have been able to save them both. . .'

'So you plunged into SIDS research to try and find the answers,' said Lissa.

'Yes. As though fate was taking a hand, I heard of this consultant's job in Melbourne which also involved setting up a SIDS research unit at the SCG. It was a chance to get away from Perth, so I applied for it and got it.'

'But surely working in that area only makes it all worse?' Lissa queried. 'I've felt your frustration when you've spoken about it, but I never dreamed you'd had personal experience.'

'It isn't something one wants to talk about. I'm trying—rather unsuccessfully—to forget.' He crossed the the buffet and poured himself another drink. 'Yes, the research is frustrating, because we still don't know why one baby in every five hundred dies unexpectedly, but at least I'm doing something. I'm trying to find out. If I can help find the cause, or one of the causes, then Natasha will not have died in vain. There are glimmers of hope, Lissa. We're getting somewhere.'

'So many causes have been put forward, one wonders if regarding SIDS as a single entity is justified.'

'I agree. There's a certain amount of chaos, and too often just another theory is identified in the Press as a "breakthrough". That's what people want to hear, of course. The fact is that infants may die suddenly of a number of causes and some of those may be attributed to SIDS when they're not classic cases of the syndrome.

For instance, it may be significant that most babies who die have had a slight cold prior to death, but so far there's no conclusive evidence as to how this contributes, if indeed it does.'

He paced to the window, turned and came quickly back. 'We don't even know if there's an answer to find,' he said. 'It may be that cot death is something that can't be predicted, or prevented, one of the random quirks of nature with which we shall have to continue to live. But that's a pessimistic view. I happen to think we will find an answer, or answers, eventually. . .and once we fully understand the mechanisms of the syndrome. . .' He stared into his glass reflectively as though continuing the train of thought in silence.

'I'm glad you're optimistic, not pessimistic,' Lissa said.

Hugo swallowed the rest of his whisky. His glance was wry. 'Scientific research is by definition optimistic.'

He moved away again, and she longed for some way to help, to ease the torment he was still going through. There was so much she wanted to say to comfort him, but she held back. She had invaded his privacy too much already.

Hugo suddenly turned back to her and demanded harshly, 'Well? Aren't you dying to tell me to pull myself together and get on with living a normal life? A few hearty clichés would be in order, wouldn't they?'

Lissa was shocked. 'Is that what you want? I'd have thought you'd have have had more than enough of that already.'

Her spirited response seemed to disconcert him. 'Yes,' he said wearily. 'And the truth is I should have pulled myself together long ago.' He glared at her as though she had accused him. 'Weakness isn't a trait I admire in others. Wallowing in self-pity is not very professional, is it?'

Lissa ached for him. 'Hugo, you're too harsh with yourself. Just because you're a doctor it doesn't mean you can't suffer like anybody else.'

'But I should be better able to rationalise a situation,' he said.

'Maybe it's better sometimes just to let things take their course.'

'It's been five years! There are some things time doesn't cure. I held Annabel in my arms and I fell to pieces inside all over again. Fathers aren't supposed to grieve like that!'

'Oh, what rot!' Lissa exclaimed. 'Men are just as emotional and sensitive as women, but they're taught to hide it. There's nothing wrong with you.'

His expression was haunted. 'Yes, there is, Lissa.'

'Well, maybe expecting a total cure for yourself is expecting too much.'

He looked startled at this remark, and his mouth twisted again in that wry half-smile. 'You can't possibly understand.'

'I know that,' she said humbly. She studied the pattern on the carpet, biting her lip. It was presumptuous of her even to offer sympathy. 'I'd better go,' she said dully, and stood up.

Hugo touched her arm as she moved away, halting her. 'Lissa. . .'

'Yes?'

His eyes moved slowly across her face, as he said quietly, 'We've both endured somewhat of an emotional experience, so what about restoring proper prespectives by having that dinner with me which you declined a while back?' A faint, challenging smile tilted his mouth as his eyes searched her face. 'Unless, of course, you have a date,' he added stiffly.

'No, I haven't.'

'You wouldn't find it too gloomy to eat with me?'

Lissa smiled. 'Of course not. But are. . .? I mean, today. . .'

'. . .is the anniversary of the death of my child. That doesn't mean I can't take out to dinner someone who sympathises and who might just distract me a little. That was what I had intended, to apologise for what must have seemed very peculiar behaviour to you, and offer food as recompense. It isn't good for me to brood, Lissa. I know that, but I do it. I know I should put it all behind me, but I can't. One day, perhaps. . .'

'I think it shows a lot of courage to continue as a paediatrician after what you went through. Every day must remind you.' Lissa wanted to hold him, comfort him, take away the pain, but she sat immobile, knowing she could not presume. He didn't want that from her.

'I nearly did change course,' he said quietly. 'for a while I couldn't even face other people's children, couldn't bear to look at them, especially babies, but I knew I had to face up to it. I like working with children, it's one of the most rewarding areas of medicine. I didn't want to give it up.'

'You're marvellous with the children,' Lissa said admiringly. 'Most of the time no one would ever guess.'

'But today I gave myself away,' he said regretfully, and with a half-amused look at her. 'You're too perceptive, Lissa. You saw what I've always taken great pains to hide. That's why I felt I owed you an explanation.'

'Thank you for that.'

'Now, let's go and enjoy our dinner.' His mood seemed to lighten as though the past minutes had lifted a burden from his shoulders. Lissa certainly felt that a weight had gone from hers.

'I—I'm not dressed for going out,' she said, contrasting her casual gear with his well-cut lightweight suit. 'I'll have to change.'

He smiled, a more normal smile than she'd ever seen before. 'I'm sure you won't take long. I'll drive you home—I don't mind waiting.'

This wasn't how she had expected the evening to turn out, Lissa thought a few minutes later, as she dashed into the shower again to freshen up, then quickly slipped into a dark blue linen dress and matching sandals. She brushed her hair out loosely and let it tumble casually around her face and on to her shoulders. It was a warm evening, so she took only a lightweight paisley shawl to slip around her shoulders if needed. She was ready in less than half an hour.

Hugo looked her over appreciatively when she re-entered the living-room of the flat, where he was idly flipping through a magazine while he waited for her. He stood up and caught hold of her hands. 'You look lovely,' he said simply. 'I haven't seen you with your hair down before.'

Embarrassed by the sudden heightening of her feelings, Lissa hurried him to the door. She wasn't sure whether she was alive or in heaven. She was going out with Hugo Stanfield! It was unbelievable. But, she cautioned herself as they went downstairs to the car, she must be careful not to read too much into this evening, as she had once before. The last time he had taken her out to dinner had been merely an impromptu farewell gesture, and this time it was only an apology for showing his feelings too strongly today. She owed him more for insulting him, but perhaps, she thought hopefully, her company would distract him a little.

It was a few minutes before she realised they were driving out of town. She turned to Hugo, who had spoken little since they'd left her flat. 'Where are we going?'

'A little place I know that has charm as well as good food. Have you been to the Mallee Root?'

'No, it sounds intriguing! What's a mallee root?'

'The root of a kind of gum tree. It grows in the Mallee—you've heard of that part of north-western Victoria?' Lissa nodded and he went on, 'It grows elsewhere too. Mallee trees are medium-sized and grow with several trunks and an umbrella top. The roots are gnarled and hard and good for burning in open fires.'

'I hope they haven't got one going tonight,' said Lissa, trying to sound as though everything was perfectly normal. 'It's still very warm.' It was, however, very comfortable in the air-conditioned car.

Hugo said, 'There's a huge open fireplace, and they do have log fires in winter. The restaurant is air-conditioned in summer.' His words were slow-paced and he sounded preoccupied. He had been put through an emotional wringer today, Lissa reminded herself, and she had made it worse. That he had been going to apologise to *her*, and was now taking her out to dinner, showed what an extraordinary man he was. How could she help loving such a man?

Sensing that he would probably prefer not to talk about medical matters, Lissa debated what topic to introduce. Or should she remain silent while they drove and leave it to him to make conversation? She decided to let the conversation flow from him, and contented herself with looking out of the car window at the unfamiliar suburbs they were driving through in the gathering dusk.

It was dark when they arrived at the Mallee Root restaurant which was tucked away in a rural corner of the foothills of the Dandenong Ranges. A path winding through tall eucalypts and tree ferns brought them to a mellow stone building with a shingle roof and wide veranda. It was an old homestead which had been converted to a restaurant, Hugo told her.

'It's the sort of house I wouldn't mind living in,' she confessed, admiring it. 'Not that I'm ever likely to be able to afford such a dream home!'

'I dare say you'll marry someone who will,' Hugo said with a touch of dryness.

Lissa let the remark pass. She followed him into the restaurant and to a table in a corner by a window. The dining-room was not crowded and there was only a low hubbub of voices mingling with the soft background music. She was amazed at the fireplace.

'I've never seen one so huge,' she exclaimed. 'Not even English inglenooks are as big as that!'

'The original owners had a few grandiose ideas,' Hugo told her.

Afterwards, Lissa could never remember what she ate for dinner that night, except that it had been delicious. Her whole mind had been focused on Hugo Stanfield, sitting opposite her as he had that time months ago just before she had flown back to England. Only that time it had been in a small Italian café, not an upmarket restaurant like this one. She didn't even remember much of what they had talked about, only that, to her surprise and pleasure, they seemed to have a few tastes in common. Hugo had seemed a little sceptical when she'd claimed to like classical music, and even more when she confessed to being a failed ballet dancer.

'I suppose you would have demonstrated your talents at the hospital Christmas fund-raiser last December,' he said, 'if you'd been here.'

She nodded gaily. 'I did the previous year. Pirouetting with a bedpan isn't as easy as you might think!'

'Tutu and all?' His eyes were mocking.

'Absolutely. Paul Norris wrote a very funny skit in verse to the music of *The Nutcracker* and *Swan Lake*. It was a terrific take-off of nurses, doctors and patients.'

'No doubt as libellous as such skits usually are.'

'Was it a good show last Christmas?'

'Very. A lot of the SCG's staff have more than medical talent.' He looked at her with interest. 'Why did you give up the ballet to become a nurse?'

'I just wasn't good enough. By the age of fourteen I knew I wasn't ever going to become a ballerina and I wasn't even sure I wanted to be, so I set my sights on another career and eventually decided that nursing was what I wanted to do. And travel. I also discovered that sport appealed more than dancing.' Lissa laughed lightly. 'It's as energetic but not as strenuous, not if you do it for fun. You can't dance for fun, you have to give it your body and soul.'

'I'm afraid I'm not very sport-minded,' Hugo said, with the faintest distaste. 'I'm not even a fanatical spectator.'

'You ought to do some exercise,' Lissa said earnestly. 'Do you jog?'

He grimaced. 'No. But I walk a lot.'

'So do I. Every morning if I can, except in winter

when I'm a bit lazy, and depending what shifts I'm on. The middle shift is best because I don't have to get up so early.'

He astonished her then by saying, 'I've seen you once or twice, in the park.'

Lissa was momentarily hurt because he must have avoided her. She said, 'I've never seen you.'

'The times I saw you, you looked engrossed in whatever was blasting your eardrums. I confess I imagined rock music; don't tell me it was *Giselle* after all.'

Lissa didn't mind the mockery. His face was more expressive now, and she felt she *was* distracting him. 'I'm rather fond of jazz for walking to. I do like rock-'n'-roll, but in discos, not to walk to.' At least, she thought, he had wondered what her taste in music was! 'Don't you play any sport at all?' she asked, determined to keep the conversation well away from minefields.

'Only golf.'

'Oh. . .' Golf was the one sport that had never greatly appealed to her.

He chuckled. 'It's a very relaxing game and involves a lot of walking. You should try it some time. I'm sure you'd have a formidable swing.'

Lissa pulled a face. 'I don't think golf is for me.' She grinned teasingly at him. 'I'm glad you didn't say lawn bowls, though!'

'I see. You're more for adventurous sports, is that it? Such as?'

'I've just learned to windsurf and I go horse-riding sometimes. I'm in the hospital netball team and I play tennis and swim and surf when I can. I ski'd last winter at Mount Buffalo. I like cross-country skiing, it's marvellous, you really ought to try it. None of that's very adventurous really. I have no yearning to drive racing cars, but I rather fancy hang-gliding and scuba-diving.'

Hugo seemed quite shocked by her catalogue. 'You make me feel exhausted! I will confess only to a sneaking desire to go ballooning.'

'Ballooning!' Lissa exclaimed. 'Oh, that's great fun. I've been up once, as a passenger only. It's not really a sport, is it, more a hobby. My friend Jacqui Brent is married to a man who goes ballooning, up at Maneroo. He pilots at weekends for a local company offering tourist flights. David used to fly gliders too.' She paused, and because Hugo was watching her intently, she rattled on to hide the fact that his dark gaze, his faintly smiling mouth, were disconcerting her quite alarmingly. 'Jacqui used to be a nurse at the SCG, you know. She would have left before you came, about the middle of last year. She got a job in a country hospital. I thought she was mad, a city girl like her, but it worked out wonderfully for her. She married David, a doctor at the Maneroo Hospital. His name's Dr Darling—isn't that terrible? Jacqui says he's used to it, and she's getting quite used to it now herself. They're going to have a baby, last I heard. I must try and get a long weekend and go up and see them. She doesn't often get down to Melbourne. She's still nursing for the time being. . .' She ran down, feeling suddenly that she must be boring him. 'Sorry, you can't possibly be interested in such trivia. . .'

He tilted the bottle of wine towards her glass, but Lissa covered it with her hand. The wine, a beautiful tangy Chardonnay, was already making her talk too much. What a silly prattler he must think her!

Hugo topped up his own glass and replaced the bottle in the ice-bucket. 'On the contrary, I'm very interested. To take one's first balloon flight with people you know would be reassuring. Perhaps I could come along some weekend when you go up to Maneroo?'

Lissa nearly slid under the table with surprise. Hugo Stanfield inviting himself to go away for the weekend with her! It was beyond her wildest dreams. It was sheer magic.

'Er—yes, I'm sure David would be delighted to take you ballooning,' she said, covered with confusion now. 'Let me know when and I'll try to organise my break to suit.' Her heart was hammering wildly. It was just unbelievable that he could want to have her company for a whole weekend. Or was it only because she could arrange a trip in a balloon for him? Soberly, she reminded herself that wishful thinking was the short road to heartbreak.

And when Hugo drove her home, and was silent for most of the way as when they had come, she told herself not to read anything into tonight, or a possible weekend at Maneroo.

Hugo accompanied her to the entrance to her block of flats. Lissa was tempted to invite him in for coffee, but afraid he might misinterpret her motive. She didn't want to frighten him off by being pushy.

'Thank you for a lovely evening,' she said. 'I didn't deserve it, but I enjoyed it immensely.'

'You deserved it,' he said quietly, and, grasping her arms lightly, bent his head and kissed her. While Lissa, dizzy with joy, almost fainted, he let go and stepped back as though he had done something unplanned and regrettable. He said in a slightly embarrassed tone, 'It might be just as well not to mention that we've been out together. You know how hospitals gossip.'

'I'm not about to encourage them to gossip about me,' said Lissa. 'Or you.'

He reached out and ran his fingers through her hair. 'You're a lovely girl, Lissa, and I enjoyed your company tonight. I would enjoy taking you out again some time. . .' There was a heavy pause before he finished '. . .so long as you didn't take it too seriously.'

Lissa's heart plunged into her shoes. With some difficulty she managed to remain light and bright as she said, 'I don't take any man very seriously, Hugo. I enjoy my freedom too much.'

He smiled, letting his fingers curl around her ear so that she tingled with a swift erotic pleasure. 'I rather thought as much.'

He bent and kissed her lightly again, his hand sliding across her nape and spreading the delicious feeling that the light touch of his fingers evoked. Then he said a swift goodnight, but not until he had seen that she was safely inside the building did he leave.

Lissa floated up to the flat in a dream. Maggie was in bed asleep and did not wake as Lissa moved quietly about in her own room. It had been an evening to remember, she thought, stretching out on cool sheets, still tasting Hugo's mouth on her lips, but she must keep her feet firmly on the ground.

Hugo didn't want people to know he had taken her out. He didn't want her to get serious about him. That was as good as telling her that when Hugo Stanfield one day emerged from his cocoon of remorse and self-recrimination, it wouldn't be to fall into the arms of Nurse Lissa Moran. Of course not. It would be into the arms of someone more on his wavelength, like Dr Jayne Rossney.

I bet she plays golf, Lissa thought dismally. She buried her head in the pillow and stuffed her fingers in her ears because her mind had suddenly started chanting again, Love me, not Jayne.

CHAPTER FIVE

IT WAS not until her morning break next day that Lissa had a moment alone with Warren. He had glanced at her with questioning concern on her arrival, but with other nurses there during briefing, he could not say anything. Later he called her aside. 'When you go for your break, bring your coffee into my office, Lissa.'

She did, and plunged straight in. 'I apologised.' Warren was obviously wondering when, so she saw no harm in telling the truth. 'He happened to mention once that he lives quite near me, so I went round last night on the off chance he'd be in, and he was.' Warren's eyebrows shot up in surprise and Lissa added, 'I wanted to get it over with.'

Warren nodded approvingly, smiling. 'And he didn't throw you out?'

'No. He was very gracious about it. He said he was, in fact, going to apologise to me and tell me why he'd reacted so strongly. He asked me not to tell anyone else. I told him you wouldn't have told me what you knew but for the circumstances.'

Warren looked relieved. 'Well, I'm glad to hear it worked out all right, Lissa.' He didn't press her to elaborate on the story as a result of what Hugo had told her personally, and Lissa did not offer any details. Nor did she tell him that Hugo had driven her out to the hills for dinner, that they hadn't got home until after midnight and that he had kissed her. That, she

thought, would no doubt have sent his eyebrows shooting right up through his hairline!

In any case, it probably would never happen again.
Like the first time, last night had been an unusual
occasion. And as for Hugo's professed desire to go
ballooning, that had probably been voiced on the spur
of the moment, and he had no intention of taking her
up on it. He'd made it very clear that he didn't want
any involvement, so he was bound to shy away from
the idea when he reflected on it.

Hugo did not come into the wards that day. It was
not the day for his weekly round, and at other times he
came only when requested for consultation over a
patient, or when he was particularly concerned to
personally monitor the progress of a child. A good deal
of his time was spent overseeing the SIDS Advice and
Counselling Service and the Research Unit.

Lissa was glad in a way. She still felt shaken from
last night's events, and emotionally drained as a result
of having discovered what a terrible, if unwitting, gaffe
she had made, and then having to drum up the courage
to apologise. She had also not quite come down to
earth after going out with Hugo and being kissed by
him, albeit most chastely. Given the normal state of
her feelings for him, she was in more turmoil than
ever.

'Come back, all is forgiven!' Karyn was waving a
hand in front of her eyes as Lissa paused while they
were setting up the medications trolley together.

Lissa jerked out of her reverie. 'What?'

'You were daydreaming! Way off the planet there
for a minute, and by the silly smile on your face you
weren't just wondering if you'd turned the gas off this

morning. Don't tell me Paul's punctured your armour at last.'

Lissa was annoyed with herself. She pulled herself together sharply. 'Sorry—I drifted for a second. I had a late night last night, and I guess I'm a bit tired.'

Karyn gave her a curious look. 'So it was Paul?'

'No, it wasn't.' Lissa sought for a way to stop the inquisition. 'I was—er—reading until late—a new book on SIDS. I'll lend it to you when I've finished. It's very comprehensive.' At least it was true she did have such a book, but it had been two nights ago that she'd stayed up late reading it.

Karyn took up the subject. 'Thanks, I'd appreciate that. It's a real mystery, isn't it? I wonder if they'll ever discover how to prevent it. There's so much publicity, you'd think it would make all parents nervous at least for the first year of their baby's life. I know it can happen later, but most cases are in the first twelve months and more in the first six than any other time. What I think must be difficult is deciding to have another child after you've lost one that way.'

Lissa checked off the last prescription sheet, but did not immediately wheel the trolley out into the ward. She waited for Karyn to lock the drugs cupboard, saying, 'That's why we sometimes have anxious parents bringing babies in the minute they think they're seeing some unusual symptom. You can't blame them for being ultra-nervous. But if you can't find anything specific wrong, what can you do but send them home again?'

'Even those electronic nursery monitors are not a hundred per cent effective,' Karyn commented. 'I believe they're widely used in the States.'

'Yes, I read that too. But the trouble is most of them

are monitoring babies who won't die from SIDS anyway. No one can prove how many lives might have been saved.' Lissa glanced over the trolley, checking that everything needed was there. She smoothed down her cover-up; it was one with a pattern of pink elephants which always made her smile. She said, 'You take a lot of risks when you have children, and SIDS is just one of them. I wouldn't let the risks put me off having a family, would you?'

Karyn smiled wickedly. 'You *are* getting clucky! There's something in the wind, isn't there?'

'No, of course there isn't!'

Karyn's look was sceptical. 'All right, I won't probe. I'll just wait patiently for the announcement. And to answer your question—no, I wouldn't either. The odds in favour of having healthy babies are greater nowadays than they've ever been. I'm glad we're not living in the Victorian era.'

'With Florence Nightingale as our DN!' laughed Lissa, and Karyn snorted.

She glanced at the clock on the wall. 'Come on, we'd better go. I've got to do Merle's feeds too today. She's got a domestic crisis, so she had to stay home with one of the children.'

'Let's hope we don't have any crises here today,' said Lissa. 'I want to get the playroom straightened out. Warren gave me some new posters and mobiles and a stack of books that one of Pinocchio's Friends brought in. The books need covering and the toys are in chaos. Some bright spark tipped all the Lego into the building blocks box.'

'You're a nurse, not a kindergarten aide!'

Lissa laughed. 'Oh, I enjoy all the peripheral activities. It's all part of nursing children, though, Karyn.

But what I intend to do is motivate a couple of our staying-in mothers. The current bunch look a bit lost, and they need something constructive to do. And one or two of those troublesome older children who are bored out of their minds can lend a hand.'

By lunchtime Lissa had organised the playroom working bee, and was satisfied that the work could be done without much supervision from her. One of the mothers, she discovered, was in fact a kindergarten teacher who had given up work when she had her first child, and she was delighted to take over the playroom. Lissa was just as delighted to offload the job and she went to lunch feeling confident that Amanda Price would restore order without delay. The last she'd seen was two of the most fractious older children eagerly accepting instructions on how to cover the books with plastic film.

Lissa ate her lunch alone. One or two colleagues stopped for a few words, but no one from her floor was there to join her. The doctors ate in their own dining-room mostly, although some of the younger ones strayed into the canteen occasionally, especially if they wanted to see particular nurses off the wards. Complete integration at mealtimes had not yet come to the SCG. So Lissa could relax, knowing she was unlikely to see Hugo coming through the door.

She still felt a little uneasy about their next encounter, although not as badly as she might have done had she not apologised to him. It was just that last night seemed so unreal and she had the awful feeling that she was going to behave stupidly when they did meet. She would probably blush and fumble with words or do something utterly silly like handing him a spatula when he wanted a speculum. How could she continue to keep her real feelings concealed now? It would be so humiliating if he guessed she was already in love with him. However, no doubt plenty of women had had crushes on him, so he was probably used to adulation and therefore might be oblivious to it now. She fervently hoped so.

She arrived back on the ward to find a flurry of activity over a new arrival who had just come up from the casualty department for urgent admission and the possibility of imminent surgery.

'Suspected acute appendicitis,' Warren told Lissa. 'But A & E aren't certain. You know how tricky diagnosis can be in some cases. Nine-year-old boy. He's been complaining of abdominal pain since he woke up this morning, according to his mother, but it didn't seem too severe, so she thought it was just a tummy upset when he vomited a couple of times. But he has a temperature now and the pains are worse.'

As he was speaking, Paul Norris arrived in a hurry. 'Emergency?' he queried.

'Yes. In Room Two.' Warren turned back to Lissa. 'You'd better come along.'

The boy's worried-looking mother sat by the bed holding her son's hand, but he seemed too listless to be anxious about his strange surroundings and the people gathered around his bed. Paul questioned her closely about symptoms as he palpated the child's abdomen and asked him if and where it was tender, then he stepped back to confer with Warren.

'See if you can get hold of Hugo, will you, Warren? I'm not too sure about this one. It's not in my opinion a simple pelvic appendix, more likely retrocaecal. Or could even be mesenteric adenitis,' he added thoughtfully. 'We might need to do a laparotomy.'

The boy's mother looked confused. 'Isn't it appendicitis, doctor?' Her expression said she feared something worse.

Paul came back to the bedside. 'Most probably, but to make sure we might just have to do a couple of tests first to rule out other possibilities.' He smiled reassuringly at the boy, 'Nothing to worry about, young man. It won't hurt.'

There was a light knock at the door and Karyn looked in. 'Mrs Cooper's husband is on the phone,' she said.

Paul glanced at her. 'Do you want to go and talk to him? Mark will be quite all right, won't you? Just for a few minutes, while Mummy tells Daddy you're going to be OK.'

Mrs Cooper seemed reluctant to leave her son, but she was also clearly anxious to reassure her husband. She went out with Karyn. Paul drew Lissa to one side and spoke quietly.

'Frequent micturition could mean a urinary tract infection, and I wouldn't rule out renal disease. However, I'll still plump for retrocaecal appendix, but I expect Hugo will want a rectal swab, a urine specimen, and he'll probably ask for a white cell count.'

Lissa was trying to concentrate on the job in hand and not think personal thoughts about Hugo whom she was now about to see. 'I'll lay up the examination trolley right away,' she said, and turned to go. As she reached the door, Hugo came in.

He looked hard at her for a moment, his face expressionless, greeted her perfunctorily and then gave all his attention to Paul and the patient. Lissa, pushing her personal feelings to one side, hurried out to lay up the examination trolley, including the equipment needed for the tests Hugo was certain to require.

After Hugo's examination of the patient was completed and Lissa had taken samples for testing and sent them down to Pathology for urgent attention, she found herself for a moment alone with Paul.

He said with some satisfaction, 'Hugo agrees it looks like a retrocaecal.'

'That means surgery straight away?' Lissa queried.

'Yes. It could be dangerous if perforated. Don't worry the Coopers, though, not at this stage.' As he spoke, Hugo came out of Mark's room. He hesitated, looking at them for a speculative moment, then said to Lissa, 'You'd better give the boy a pre-med right away.'

Looking at him, Lissa felt an intense longing to reach up and kiss him and entwine her arms around his neck. Instead she hurried off to do his bidding.

She went down to the operating suite with the very nervous Mrs Cooper, chatting to her and the boy as reassuringly as she knew how. It had been a bit of a shock to both of them, the boy being taken ill so suddenly. Mrs Cooper pretended to be normal, but Lissa guessed how anxious she was and made sure that she stayed with her son as long as possible. She explained to Mark exactly what was going to happen and praised him for being brave.

'I expect you'll be allowed into the recovery-room when he comes round,' Lissa said, settling his mother in an ante-room with coffee and a magazine. Mrs Cooper had said she wasn't hungry enough to have lunch in the cafeteria, but she agreed to let Lissa send for some sandwiches.

Back on the ward Lissa found that Mr Cooper had arrived, bringing an overnight bag. Lissa took him down to his wife and left them together after offering a few more words of reassurance. By the time Mark had had his operation and been returned to the ward, she would be off duty.

Before she finished for the day she went along to the playroom to see how the re-establishment of order was progressing.

'Hey, it looks fantastic!' she exclaimed, delighted with the transformation. Already the shelves were tidier, and the new posters had been pinned up. The two mothers looked pleased and were obviously glad to have something to occupy them. The children who were covering the new books were quietly engaged at a table, concentrating hard, and for once no one was bothering to watch television.

Lissa felt even more tired than usual when she reached home. It had not been a specially hectic day— only one emergency was a very good day—but emotionally she still felt drained. Her feelings had been in conflict at first because she hadn't expected to see Hugo, then in turmoil because events had made it necessary to, but in circumstances where they had not exchanged one personal word. She couldn't help agonising over what he might be thinking about last night. Did he regret telling her so much about his wife and baby? Did he regret taking her out to dinner? And, most of all, did he regret that small intimacy as he said goodnight? Lissa was sure the answer was yes on all counts. Nothing in his manner that day had encouraged her to think otherwise.

The next day was Saturday, but Lissa was working. She had Sunday off, but when, encountering her in the lift as she was going on duty, Paul invited her to play tennis at a friend's house, she declined.

He looked quizzical. 'I thought you were anxious to have your revenge on me for the last match we played.'

'I am! But I have a lot of chores to catch up on. I think I'll stay in for once.' Whether he sensed it was merely an excuse, she couldn't tell, but the truth was she just didn't feel like Paul's company for a whole day. It would be too much of a strain. Paul was nice, but at the moment her thoughts were too difficult to wrench away from Hugo. She felt she needed a little time and space to restore a more balanced outlook.

She must not let things grow out of proportion, she told herself, as she tied the strings on a pink cover-all with an appliquéd joey peeping out of his mother's pouch which was a pocket. The other night had been an incident, that was all, time out, but it was of no significance. Nothing further was going to occur. Hugo's silence was intended to make sure she realised that.

Warren was off, so Lissa was in charge. She was very glad to find the young boy who had been admitted the previous day looking a great deal better than he had before surgery. His father had stayed the night with him and seemed amazed at the rapid recovery of his son after the appendicectomy.

'Oh, I expect he'll be allowed up while we make his bed later on, and tomorrow he'll be able to get up and play.' Lissa smiled at the boy. 'It wasn't so bad, was it?'

'It was funny,' said Mark, his face crinkling up. 'I was talking to the doctor and there was this little prick in the back of my hand, and then I woke up somewhere else.'

'That was the anaesthetic,' Lissa told him. 'It's amazing how swiftly it works, isn't it?'

We'd love you to accept 4 Best Sellers, a cuddly teddy bear plus a surprise Mystery Gift - all absolutely FREE!

Best Sellers are a very special Mills & Boon series, in which we re-publish some of the most popular romances published over the years. They are very much for the connoisseur of Romance; the discerning reader who appreciates all that's finest in the modern love story.

And when you read your marvellous free books, you've got something else to look forward to...

Every other month you can go on to receive the 4 latest Best Sellers, for a very reasonable £5.40! postage and packing Free - We'll also send you a Free Newsletter featuring author news, competitions and much more!

And all this comes with no commitment, you can stop receiving books at any time, simply by writing to us.

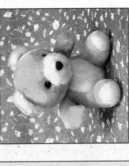

FREE TEDDY

This lovely soft teddy measuring 4½ inches sitting is yours FREE together with a surprise mystery gift.

4 Classic Love Stories ABSOLUTELY —FREE!—

BOOKS LIKE THESE

Reader Service
FREEPOST
P.O. Box 236
Croydon
Surrey
CR9 9EL

FREE BOOKS & GIFTS CLAIM

EXTRA BONUS

Yes Please send me my 4 free books and 2 free gifts - and reserve me a special Reader Service Subscription. If I decide to subscribe I shall look forward to receiving 4 superb Best Sellers every other month for just £5.40 postage and packing absolutely free. If I decide not to subscribe, I shall write to you within 10 days. The free books and gifts will be mine to keep in any case. I understand that I am under no obligation whatsoever - I can cancel or suspend my subscription at any time simply by writing to you.
I am over 18 years of age.   **12AOB**

We all love surprises so as well as the **FREE** books and teddy bear, here's an intriguing mystery gift especially for you - no clues send off today.

NAME _____

ADDRESS _____

_____

_____ POSTCODE _____

SIGNATURE _____

SEND NO MONEY NOW - TAKE NO RISKS

'I thought I was in outer space,' said Mark seriously. 'I thought I was waking up on another planet. Everything looked so strange, and I felt dizzy. Then I saw Dad. . .'

Mr Cooper put in, 'He said, "Dad, how did we get here?" and I said, "By ambulance," and he said, "That's a silly name for a space-ship!"'

Lissa laughed. 'Sometimes the anaesthetic makes you imagine funny things. How's your wife, Mr Cooper?'

'She's greatly relieved, Sister. We've got one of the little ones down with bronchitis, unfortunately, so this happened at an awkward time. But Mark's been very brave and he says he doesn't mind being in hospital by himself. I won't need to stay in tonight. We'll be in to see him tomorrow, of course.'

'You won't have to stay in hospital for long, Mark,' Lissa told him. 'Only a few days, I expect. We'll see what Dr Norris and Dr Stanfield say. I bet you're one of the best patients and the quickest to recover they've had in a long while.'

Shortly afterwards both Paul and Hugo visited the boy, but although there was an opportunity, as Paul was bleeped and had to rush off, Hugo did not linger, and his exchanges with Lissa were impersonal and characteristically brusque. They were back to square one, she thought. Well, not quite. Never again would she let him rile her, never again would she come back with a sharp retort. For as long as she lived, Hugo's personal agony would haunt her.

On Sunday morning, Lissa was still in bed when the security phone buzzed about eight o'clock. Maggie had gone away for the weekend with Henry, so Lissa was

alone. She decided to ignore the summons, but who-
ever it was was insistent. Surely it wasn't Paul, to try
and persuade her to play tennis after all. Reluctantly,
she got out of bed and padded into the hallway and
lifted the receiver.

'Yes, who is it?'

Lissa nearly dropped the receiver when a male voice
said, 'Hugo.'

'Hugo!' she squeaked.

'Did I get you out of bed?'

'Er—well, yes, as a matter of fact.' She added
defensively, 'It is only eight o'clock.'

'Sorry. It's a beautiful day, which you may not have
noticed yet, and I'm playing golf. I just thought I'd
drop by and see if you'd care to have a lesson.'

He sounded nonchalant, even offhand, but her heart
was racing like an express train. 'Golf. . .' She repeated
dully. She didn't recall expressing any desire to take
lessons.

'I know it's not your favourite sport, but I thought
maybe if you tried you might change your mind.'

She didn't understand. Why was he doing this?
Because he saw her as 'safe' company? Or was it
because if he took her out a few times, he'd feel better
about imposing on her friends to go ballooning?

Did she want to go? she asked herself. Well, of
course she did. What mattered was whether it was wise
to go. Every hour she spent with him off duty was
likely to make the inevitable heartbreak more
agonising.

'Can I come up?' he was saying.

She glimpsed herself in the hall mirror, tousled hair,
flimsy nightdress, no make-up. What a mess! 'I'm not
dressed,' she murmured.

A soft chuckle breezed into her ear. 'If that worries you, open the door and go and get dressed. I'll wait for you as I did the other night.'

It was madness. She didn't want to learn to play golf. But she did want to be with Hugo. 'All right.' She pressed the button to let him through the street door, and flipped the latch on the flat door. Then she fled back to her bedroom. She flung off her nightclothes and dashed into the bathroom. She heard the front door click as she closed the bathroom door. When she emerged a few minutes later, there was an unexpected aroma in the flat. Coffee!

Lissa pulled on a pair of white culottes and a scarlet shirt which was the only ironed one in her wardrobe. She knotted a red and white scarf around the collar, then laced on her white trainers, which were reasonably clean. She plaited her hair and pinned the plait to the top of her head, applied a discreet amount of mascara to her lashes, then, feeling decidedly bemused, went out to greet her visitor. She found him in the kitchen, wielding a knife over a loaf.

'Toast?' he demanded.

'Er—yes, please.' She laughed in amazement. Dr Stanfield *was* a little arrogant, you couldn't get away from that, the sort of man to take over all kinds of situations, but domesticity was not a role Lissa had imagined for him, especially not in someone else's kitchen. He was certainly full of surprises. Enigmatic men were bound to be, she supposed. 'You have made yourself at home! The coffee smells wonderful. Why doesn't it smell like that when I make it?'

'Oh, men know more about making coffee than women do,' he said, straight-faced.

'Chauvinist! I suppose they know more about cutting bread and making toast too.'

'I never burn toast,' he announced gravely. 'Can you honestly say that?' Was that a twinkle in the dark brooding eyes? Lissa felt crumbly inside. Was this the same man who had seemed to look through her yesterday, the man she was certain had regretted taking her out to dinner? She still couldn't quite believe that he was in her kitchen, making breakfast for her.

'No, I can't,' she admitted, perching on a stool at the small breakfast bar. 'But you didn't have to get breakfast for me.' She regarded the array of cereals, jams and fruit before her with amusement.

'I didn't want you skipping it. Golf requires more energy than I expect you realise. If you can be concerned for my health, then surely I can be concerned for yours?'

'I see. Retaliation because I said you should exercise.'

'Not exactly.' He let his smile broaden a little. 'Your cereal cupboard looks like a supermarket shelf. I wasn't sure which one you had earmarked for Sundays.'

'I have muesli every day,' she told him. 'The rest are Maggie's. She likes variety.'

'And you don't?' He seemed to be referring to more than breakfast cereals.

'Variety is the spice of life,' she said lightly, 'especially in some things, like sport, for instance.'

'And men?'

Lissa looked for a teasing glance, but his head was turned away. She took refuge in flippancy.

'That's what Women's Liberation is all about. Same rules for us as for the men.' That should reassure him, she thought.

'Orange juice?' he asked. 'I see you have some in the fridge.'

'I usually have an orange,' she said, taking one from the bowl and starting to peel it. 'And marmalade on my toast.'

'Is your flatmate overweight?' Hugo asked as he returned the unwanted cereal packets and pots of jam to the cupboard.

'A bit. She has a rather sweet tooth, I'm afraid.'

'And not as much willpower as you.' His eyes drifted lazily over her slender figure, which he seemed to approve.

He poured coffee for them both and leaned against the sink counter to drink his while Lissa ate a bowl of muesli and the two slices of toast he'd made for her. She was so churned up she could hardly swallow, but she knew that, if she tried to get out of eating it all, Hugo was quite capable of standing over her until she did.

'Where is she, by the way?' Hugo asked. 'Sleeping in?'

'She's away for the weekend.' Lissa was glad her flatmate was not there, and no doubt Hugo was too. Not that Maggie would gossip; she worked in a distant part of the hospital anyway. If Hugo was anxious not to broadcast that he had taken Lissa out, he had taken a bit of a risk calling like this, as Maggie might well have been at home. But he would have relied on her, Lissa guessed, to ask Maggie to be discreet.

They were at the golf course by ten and by half-past Lissa was having her first lesson. She had learned the difference between the various kinds of clubs, the function of woods and irons, and a variety of terms like birdie, bogey and down the middle were flitting around her brain as she tried to concentrate.

It was hard because Hugo was so close, standing there showing her how to hold the club, his long fingers clasped over hers as they gripped the shaft, his breath warm on her neck and cheek as he explained how to hold the club correctly.

'Right, now swing it. . .' He swung with her a few times, which necessitated a delicious body contact which sent electrifying sensations through Lissa's nervous system. Then he let her do it on her own. 'Not too high. . .bend your wrists as you go into the back swing. . .' Hugo's instructions bombarded her as she sliced again and again at thin air until he was satisfied.

'Very good,' he said at last. 'You've got a natural flair. You'll need to watch your posture, though. Unless you're firm on the back foot, you won't get much power into your strokes. Now, let's try it with a ball and see how straight you can hit.' He took a tee out of his pocket and rammed it into the turf, then carefully balanced a golf ball on it.

Lissa looked at the ball, then at the club, adjusted her grip a little, and swallowed hard. She swung the club backwards, then played a stroke she was sure would send the ball for miles. It almost dislocated her shoulder. But when she recovered her balance, Hugo was standing there, hands on hips, laughing, and the ball was still on the tee. Lissa glanced at it malevolently, but was more astonished at the sound of Hugo laughing without restraint. It was a sound she hadn't heard before.

'Not bad,' he conceded. 'Try again.'

'My muscles won't stand it!'

'I thought you were fit.'

'Yes, I am!' Lissa shaped up again and this time she hit the ball, but the dull click of ball on wood meant she had topped it and it skittered only a short way without rising. Hugo retrieved it and said, 'Keep trying.'

After another few minutes of practice he decided they would go round the course.

'But I'm hopeless!' Lissa said. 'You'll make a laughing stock of me.'

'Nonsense—it's the best way to learn. I told you, you're a natural. You have a muscular fluidity that'll make you a good golfer in no time. I don't expect you to go round on par, and we'll give up as soon as you feel you've had enough.' He looked intently at her. 'We can give up now if you don't think you're going to enjoy it.'

Lissa pursed her lips. Golf had never attracted her, but the last few minutes had opened up a challenge. There was a great deal of skill required and she felt the urge to master the game after all. Besides, the golf course was wonderful, hectares of lush green grass with copses and clumps of trees, and birds flitting about. The morning was warming up, but there was a cool breeze, and she felt exhilarated already. Whether that was because of the game or the man she was with, she didn't care to analyse. She pulled out the white cotton hat she had shoved into her pocket before leaving home, and crammed it on. Hugo was wearing a cap with a visor.

'All right, let's go,' she said. 'You'll probably get fed up with me in no time. I'm bound to ruin your day.'

'I don't think you'll do that,' he answered softly. For a moment their eyes met. His were really smiling for the first time, and seeing it made Lissa's heart race.

Hugo's guard was down today. At last she was being allowed to glimpse the real man, and he was totally different from what she had imagined. The trouble was, this man was more likely to break her heart than ever. But there was no going back. She had been in love with him for too long now anyway. She could hardly blame him if he gave her new reasons for loving him.

For the first three holes, Lissa was a disaster. Many times she almost wept in chagrin and frustration as she missed hitting balls, drove them into bunkers, trees and bushes, and even lost them altogether.

'I told you I'd be hopeless!' she wailed. 'You must be regretting you ever suggested this, Hugo. Unless you're a masochist.'

'I am enjoying it immensely,' he insisted, grinning at her.

'Torturer!' she accused, grimly taking her stance again after watching him slice a ball with astonishing finesse so that it landed within easy one-shot putting distance of the next flag.

'Your hands are slipping too far down,' he told her, and corrected her error by again closing his hands over hers. It was bliss with his arms around her and his cheek brushing hers, so Lissa found it hard to concentrate on what he was saying. She could have relaxed back into his arms against that broad muscular chest with the greatest of ease.

He stepped back. 'There you go. . .it just takes practice.'

I can do this, Lissa was muttering to herself, I know I can. She hit the ball hard this time. It lifted in a high arc and hit the ground quite near the next hole. Hugo was quick to praise the shot in warm words, and with a congratulatory slap on the shoulder. He left his hand there as they walked towards the ball. Lissa had never felt happier.

By the time they had completed nine holes, it was very hot and, Hugo suggested, lunchtime.

'You didn't do badly,' he told her. 'for a raw beginner, you put on a pretty good show. You hit some lovely shots that any regular player would be proud of, and your putting is intelligent. You've got a good eye, Lissa.' His smile mocked her. 'Now, what do you think of golf?'

'I enjoyed it,' she answered truthfully. 'I think I might get hooked if I played often enough.' Which she wasn't likely to, she thought. Nobody she knew except Hugo played golf, and she was sure that today was a one-off occasion, a pay-off in advance for his ballooning weekend.

They had lunch at the clubhouse in a pleasant restaurant overlooking the course, and afterwards Hugo suggested that it was too hot to continue playing, although Lissa was willing. She guessed he had probably had enough of her amateurism, despite his kind remarks.

'I thought a swim would be the thing this afternoon,' he suggested, lifting a querying eyebrow. How could she have thought him arrogant? Lissa mused.

'It'll be terribly crowded on the Bay beaches,' she said. And there was hardly time to drive down to Lorne or Ocean Grove or one of the less crowded southern beaches.

'I was thinking of a pool,' said Hugo. 'My house has one. You can stop off and pick up a swimsuit on the way.'

Lissa's stomach contracted. It sounded as though he

was suggesting a pool party for two at his place. Would she be walking into one of the oldest traps in the world if she agreed to go? Was all this—this friendliness calculated to have one outcome only? She'd been a pushover so far, she thought, accepting his invitations without demur, so who could blame him for thinking she would be a pushover all the way?

She looked at him, watching her enigmatically, waiting for her compliance. Could she handle this? she wondered in sudden panic. If things did not turn out quite the way he expected, he would lose interest in her immediately, she was sure of that. What she wasn't sure of was whether she would have the willpower to make things turn out the way her good sense would say they ought to. Or would her feelings for Hugo take charge?

She wrestled with the problem for a few seconds, but, with those compelling dark eyes melting her bones, discovered that she was unable to say no. 'Yes, I'd love that,' she said matter-of-factly and without the slightest hint of suspicion in her voice.

CHAPTER SIX

SHE COULD still get out of it, Lissa thought, as Hugo swung the car to a halt in front of her block of flats. She could still play safe and say no to his invitation. Right now.

'I'll wait here for you,' he said.

Lissa hesitated, but she couldn't say no. That would be like insulting him again. His smile had reached his eyes at last, and the knowledge that she was responsible for that, that being with her had helped him to unbend a little, made up her mind. She slid out of her seatbelt and got out of the car.

'Shan't be long,' she said, and dashed through the entrance and up the stairs.

Because she went swimming quite a lot, Lissa owned several swimsuits. She flung them all on her bed and contemplated them thoughtfully. Which one was the most suitable? She rejected the skimpy bikinis as too provocative for this occasion and settled for a new maillot in black lycra with one wide diagonal white stripe from shoulder to thigh. She undressed and slipped it on, viewing herself critically in the mirror. With its high-cut front and low back, it was more dramatic than revealing. Nevertheless, the stretch fabric emphasised her firmly rounded breasts and the cut-away gusset drew attention to the slender shapeliness of her thighs and legs.

She slipped her culottes back on, but swapped the shirt for a loose-fitting, black and white patterned beach jacket. From the bathroom she grabbed a bottle of sunscreen, slung her sunglasses around her neck again, and as an afterthought on her way out, grabbed the container of orange juice from the fridge.

Hugo was admiring the gardens in the forecourt of the block of flats where the beds were ablaze with petunias and marigolds. 'Who looks after the garden?' he asked as she came up to him. 'Or are you lucky to have a garden-minded landlord?'

Lissa pulled a face. 'Not the landlord. We have a dear old couple on the ground floor who look after it. They like doing it. It looks fantastic, doesn't it?'

'Very nice indeed.' He was looking at her, though, as they walked back to the car. 'You're not a garden person?'

'I've never had much opportunity,' Lissa confessed. 'My dad is a rose fanatic, though, and Mum likes growing vegetables, so I suppose there might be a latent talent somewhere.' As she buckled on her seat-belt, she added, 'What about you? You've got a big garden at Rosewood Avenue. I suppose you employ a gardener.'

He nodded. 'Janet—my housekeeper, whom you met that evening you came round—and her husband live in. She looks after the house and he does the garden. But I like to potter myself when I have time. Gardening is good for helping the thought processes. It can take you out of yourself for a while. It's very relaxing.'

'I suppose so.' Lissa was thinking that with his housekeeper and her husband around, the husband possibly even working in the garden, she didn't have much to worry about.

As they went into Hugo's house, however, he mentioned casually, 'Janet and Derek are away this weekend. They have a little beach house down at Rye.'

So we're all alone, Lissa thought. Well, so what? That's not a problem. She handed him the container of orange juice. 'I didn't want to drink every drop you have,' she explained.

He took the plastic bottle, his fingers brushing hers briefly at the exchange and sending little arrows of fire along her veins. 'Go and make yourself comfortable by the pool or have a swim,' he said. 'I'll just go and change, then bring you a cold drink.'

Lissa strolled out through the french windows which he had opened, on to a wide slate-paved patio which surrounded a large in-ground swimming pool. Under a wisteria-covered pergola there was a leisure setting of white chairs, table and loungers. She stood for a moment admiring the huge rear garden. It was densely planted with trees and shrubs which concealed the adjacent houses completely. In the lawn beyond the pool there were neat beds of flowers, and on the patio large tubs overflowed with summer annuals like petunias, marigolds and salvias. It was still and quiet with the languor of a hot summer afternoon, and Lissa felt her slight tension slipping rapidly away.

She crossed the patio to the pergola, slipped out of her culottes and beach jacket, and, as Hugo had not yet put in an appearance, she decided to take a swim. The glittering water reflecting the blue tiles of the pool looked very inviting. As she dived in, she heard a telephone ringing distantly in the house.

Twenty minutes later, when Lissa clambered out, Hugo had still not come. She glanced at the upper windows of the house and wondered what was keeping him. The sun dried her rapidly and she sat down to apply sunscreen to the exposed parts of her body. She had finished all the bits she could reach when Hugo at last appeared, carrying a tray with glasses and a jug of orange juice, towels over one arm. He was wearing brief red bathing trunks, and Lissa stifled a sharp intake of breath at the sight of his almost naked male body with its taut muscles, fuzz of dark chest hair and athletic arms and legs. He looked taller and was deeply tanned and more muscular than she had expected. No doubt he got a good deal of his exercise swimming.

'I'm sorry I was so long,' he apologised, placing the tray on the table. 'Maybe you heard the phone ring?'

'Yes, I did,' she remembered. 'It's all right. I had a lovely swim.'

He straightened up, and stood looking down at her, but not in a way that might have made her feel uncomfortable. 'It was my mother. She usually rings on Sundays.' He added with a wry little smile, 'She still worries about me.' He seemed more subdued now as he held out his hand. 'Let me do the bits you can't reach.'

He took the bottle and deftly smoothed the lotion across her back and shoulders. His fingertips brushing across the hollow in the small of her back where the swimsuit dipped almost to her coccyx was tantalisingly erotic, and Lissa bit her lip to repress the tide of feeling that suddenly washed over her. It was disturbing to find herself quite so vulnerable.

'Thanks. That should do it,' she said quickly. 'I don't plan to sunbathe in full sun. It's too hot today.'

'Would you like an orange juice?' He poised the jug over a glass while looking at her. She nodded, and he poured out for both of them.

Lissa clasped her hands around the icy glass he handed her and took several long swallows. 'Mmm, that's good. What did you put in it? Besides the orange juice, I mean?' She frowned at him suspiciously, and he laughed. His mood seemed to be lightening again.

'A dash of bitters and some mineral water, that's all.'

'It's delicious. It tones down the sweetness of the orange. I'll have to try that mix myself.'

Hugo motioned to one of the loungers. 'Why don't you put your feet up? Nurses need to do that occasionally, don't they?'

Lissa moved to a lounger and stretched out. He drew up the other one beside hers, stretching out himself, hands behind his head, looking more relaxed than she'd ever seen him.

'You didn't tell me you swam for exercise,' Lissa remarked after a lengthy silence.

'It's funny, but I never think of it as exercise. We lived near the beach when I was young, and swimming was just a part of life. Like most people I tend to think of exercise as something you do because it's good for you, not for pleasure.' He laughed with a naturalness that made Lissa exult, and feel a warm inner glow because in some mysterious way she had helped to release that laughter.

'If you lived near the beach, then you must have surfed too,' she said. 'Western Australia's beaches are wonderful for surfing, aren't they?'

He nodded. 'Yes. I used to surf a lot when I was young, but I haven't done for years.' There were shadows in his voice as he went on, 'Angie didn't care for the beach. She was a redhead and burned easily. She said the beach only made her miserable.'

'Were you married long?' Lissa ventured, her curiosity about his wife making her daring.

He stared at the sky through the network of gnarled wisteria branches. 'Six years. I'd just qualified and she was still at med school when we married. We waited until we'd both finished paediatrics before we started a family. . .' His voice took on a rough edge and Lissa regretted her curiosity.

'Don't talk about it, Hugo,' she said gently, 'unless you want to.'

He half turned his head to look at her. 'It's funny, but I seem to be able to talk to you about it. I never have before.' He sat up suddenly. 'But I didn't bring you here so I could indulge in self-pity all afternoon.'

He was sitting on the edge of his lounger, facing her. 'Why *did* you bring me here?' she asked, as though the question had come from some inner place, unbidden.

He moved to the edge of her lounger, grasped the arms of it and leaned towards her. Then he cupped her face in his hands. 'For the pleasure of your company,' he said, his eyes losing their grave expression and momentarily twinkling. 'And because I wanted a nice private place in which to kiss you. All morning on the golf course, I wanted to. . .' He leaned that little bit closer to bring his lips against hers, and Lissa felt her own part slightly as a swift breath of surprise escaped.

His mouth was firm and testing, his thumbs idly stroking the hollows beneath her chin, fingertips lightly pressuring her temples. A wave of heat melted her, and her heartbeat doubled its normal rhythm. The moment when he should have lifted his mouth and ended what had been a very restrained kiss, Lissa suddenly found herself lifting her arms and crossing her wrists behind his neck.

The effect was electric. His control seemed to snap and he gathered her into his arms, flinging himself beside her on the lounger. 'Lissa. . .' he murmured huskily, dark eyes smouldering with desire. 'What are you doing to me?'

'Hugo, I. . .' She tried to frame some sort of protest, but abandoned the attempt as Hugo's mouth closed over hers, this time with a desperate need. He flung one leg across hers, holding her captive half beneath him, and for moments that seemed to go on forever she floated in a hazy world that was part bliss, part half-acknowledged apprehension.

'You're so lovely, Lissa,' he said, holding her gaze and half smiling as he pushed the straps of her swimsuit off her shoulders and exposed her breasts to cover them again with warm caressing palms. His touch was as hypnotic as the slow smouldering of his eyes and rendered her powerless. He sank back against her and teasing her taut nipple until she felt she would explode, he nuzzled into her neck, fanning her skin with a warm breath and paralysing her will as no man had done before. When his mouth could stand denial no longer, he let it travel slowly across the ridge of her collarbone, down the sweep of smooth skin to the swell of her breast and the exquisitely sensitive peak that his finger-tips had aroused and then relinquished to an even more erotic pleasure.

Once he glanced up into her face almost anxiously. 'The trouble is, kissing's not enough, is it?'

Lissa squirmed a little away from him. 'I suppose not—you're a man, after all.'

He laughed softly and ran his fingers down her side and across her bare hip, sliding them under the stretchy fabric to cup her small firm buttock as he had her breast, a strategy which enabled him to pull her purposefully back against him. 'And you're a woman—a very desirable woman, Lissa. An irresistible woman. The only woman for a long, long time who's made me feel so alive. I had thought my feelings were dead along with everything else. . .' He buried his face between her breasts and muttered in a kind of anguish, 'I want to make love to you. . . I haven't made love to a woman for more than five years.'

'Why me?' Lissa whispered.

He smiled up at her. 'I don't know. . .there must be something special about you, Lissa, something that the part of me that's been dead for so long has suddenly responded to.' He touched his lips to her mouth, her nose, her eyes, and raked his fingers helplessly through her hair. 'I'm crazy about you. . .bewitched.'

Lissa stiffened in horror and closed her eyes. No! Surely her incantations were not responsible for this? Surely Hugo had not brought her here to make love to her merely because of some overpowering compulsion engendered by her wishful thinking?

'I—I didn't realise,' she said, panicking a little. 'I shouldn't have come.'

He stroked her cheek. 'Don't tell me you and I don't, at this moment, want the same thing.'

'I don't know. . .' She struggled in his grasp and he relaxed his hold, taking his weight off her legs. 'I'm not sure.' She managed to sit up and hurriedly pulled up her swimsuit top. She felt overwhelmed by him. 'Hugo, I didn't expect. . .'

His expression was rapidly hardening. 'You mean you didn't see it as a challenge to prove you could thaw out the cold, distant, rather abrasive paediatrician who seems to have a knack of rubbing you up the wrong way?' Sarcasm sharpened his tone.

Lissa was hurt. 'Now you are being abrasive!'

He pulled her head against his shoulder. 'Sorry, I didn't mean to upset you. I'm going too fast.'

'It's not that—it's just that I—I don't know if I want this to—go any further.'

'I think you do,' he murmured softly.

She coloured deeply in her confusion. 'Hugo, I know this might sound silly, but I've never had an affair with anyone. I've never made love to anyone, and I'm not sure I want to—just for a day.'

He looked genuinely taken aback, then he was laughing softly against her shoulder. 'I confess I hadn't expected such innocence. What about all that variety-is-the-spice-of-life talk? What about Paul Norris?'

Lissa jerked her head up. 'You don't believe me?'

'Should I?'

She lowered her gaze a little, but still watched his face from under quivering lashes. 'I just said what I thought you expected, or would believe anyway. I wasn't expecting to be tested.'

He studied her face. 'I believe you. And, odd though it may seem, I'm glad you were just being glib. Believe me, Lissa, I'm not about to force myself on you. Forgive me for getting carried away.'

Already he was retreating from her, and Lissa felt the pain of regret. But she couldn't explain that she desperately wanted him to make love to her, but that she was afraid to let it happen because afterwards there would only be heartbreak. If she went on helping him to break down barriers, if she let him make love to her, that would be fine for him, but what of her? It didn't mean he would love her afterwards. Her heartbreak would be all the harder to bear. But he didn't know how she really felt about him, and that was something she could not tell him.

'I'm sorry,' she said. 'I got a bit carried away myself.'

He dragged his hands reluctantly from her. 'Let's have a swim.'

They swam desultorily for a few minutes, each requiring time to unwind, to restore their emotions to a less dangerous level. A lightness of mood gradually returned and they worked off some energy in ridiculous horseplay, in racing each other up and down the pool, until the tension had all ebbed away and the camaraderie of the morning was restored.

'That was great,' said Lissa, towelling herself vigorously after they had climbed out. She glanced at the sun which was now dipping behind the taller trees. 'I'd better be going. It's been a terrific day, Hugo. Thanks for the golfing lesson. I might just take it up some time.' She reached for her beach jacket, but he picked it up first and held it out for her. As she turned her back and slid her arms into the sleeves he folded it and his arms around her.

'You still sound very unforgiving,' he said.

'Don't be silly! I've taken up enough of your day. . .' Suddenly she was reminded of the professional gulf between them, and she felt awkward.

Hugo whirled her to face him. 'I feel a heel, as though you must think I planned to get you here and seduce you, as a sort of therapy. . .'

'Maybe that's the kind of therapy you do need,' Lissa said, trying to distance herself from him mentally. 'You've bottled up your grief and inhibitions for too long. Life has to go on, Hugo. You can't ignore it. You can't cut yourself off completely.' She bit her lip. 'I'm sorry. . . I shouldn't have said that.'

He looked distraught suddenly. 'Lissa, don't go home yet. Please! Stay a while. Let's have dinner and talk. I like the way you talk. I like the way you listen. I feel relaxed with you.' He paused, then rather shamefacedly said, 'I guess the fact is I'm lonely. I have cut myself off, buried myself in self-pity and recriminations, and it hasn't changed a thing. It's just made me a grumpy old bear. . .' A rueful smile tilted his mouth. 'We won't go out. We'll knock up something simple here and talk. . .and I promise I won't. . .' the faint smile became a grin '. . .I won't try to seduce you.'

Lissa faced him helplessly. 'If talking helps. . .'

He clamped his hands tightly on her shoulders. 'It does, Lissa, it helps a lot.'

'All right,' she murmured. She picked up her culottes and her bag. 'Is there somewhere I can change?'

'Come with me. You can have a shower and change upstairs.'

He showed her to a small guest bedroom with adjoining bathroom and provided a huge fluffy towel. 'Come down to the kitchen when you're ready,' he said, and then gripping her upper arm briefly, 'Thanks, Lissa.'

He was already in the kitchen when she came downstairs. She had washed her hair and it was still damp and clinging around her face. It would soon dry naturally. Hugo turned to greet her with a smile. He had changed into shorts and a T-shirt. 'Janet left half a dozen different salads, so you can take your choice. Do you like avocados?'

'So much so I have to ration myself!'

He squeezed the one he had removed from a bowl on top of the refrigerator. 'This one is about perfect, I'd say. Now what about olives, pickled onions, beetroot?'

'I have a healthy appetite and few dislikes,' Lissa declared. 'Can I do anything?'

'No, just take a pew and look beautiful. Shall we eat outside?'

'Why not? It's going to be a warm night.'

He placed the bowls of salad on a large tray alongside plates, cutlery and serviettes. 'Now, let's see about bread.' He investigated the bread bin and found a French stick which Lissa immediately approved of. 'Do you like garlic bread?' Hugo demanded.

'Yes, but. . .'

'Won't take a jiffy.' He sliced the loaf, buttered the slices and sprinkled them with garlic powder and pepper, then placed the bread, foil-wrapped, in the microwave. 'What would you like to drink?' he asked. 'Claret, Riesling, Chardonnay. . .?'

'I really don't mind.' She was touched by his eagerness to please her.

'What about champagne? I've got a couple of bottles of Yellow Glen chilled.'

'We're not celebrating anything, are we?' Lissa queried drily.

Hugo gave her one of his long enigmatic looks, then said, 'I think perhaps I might be.' For a moment she caught a glimpse of desire kindling again in the dark eyes that surveyed her intently, and her nerve-ends quivered. There was a deep-seated ache inside her that she couldn't exactly diagnose, except that she knew it wouldn't be there if it weren't for Hugo.

Darkness fell quickly after they had eaten. They had

been talking while they ate, mostly about the SIDS research which Hugo was engaged in. After what he had said earlier, Lissa had half expected him to talk more about his wife and daughter and the tragic circumstances of their deaths, but he didn't. He seemed to want to use her more as a sounding board for his theories versus some of the other lines of research.

'The trouble is we can't positively say that sudden infant death is due to some specific mechanism. We can't say categorically that it's due to a respiratory obstruction or cardiac arrhythmia, for instance. If we could, then we'd be seeing some real light at the end of the tunnel. As it is, there are so many avenues to investigate, it's difficult to know which to take.'

'Which line of research have you taken?' asked Lissa.

'Respiratory failure,' Hugo said, and she saw the doubt cloud his eyes.

'You must have good reason for that.'

He shrugged. 'Not much more than intuition.' He laughed hollowly. 'That doesn't sound very scientific, does it? We examined the findings of all lines of research worldwide and chose to centre ours on what we reckoned might be the most productive. The trouble was, almost all seemed equally viable. I'm very impressed with the genes theory, because that was something that haunted Angie and me. Were we to blame genetically? Was it something hereditary in us that caused the death of our baby?'

It was the first time all evening he had mentioned his personal involvement. Lissa said, 'I know there's been quite a bit published, but nothing really conclusive.'

'There are a lot of genetically induced diseases. I wouldn't discount the idea. But it seemed to us that we could possibly contribute more by branching out along the hypoxemic stress road. The unit is investigating several new hypotheses including the role of the hormone cortisol, and I think we're about to reach some interesting conclusions. . .'

'A breakthrough?' She couldn't help sounding excited.

He raised a cautionary hand. 'I would be reluctant to go that far. A further extension of our knowledge, perhaps.' He grimaced. 'The Press will call it a breakthrough, of course.' He frowned. 'All this is naturally strictly confidential.'

'Absolutely.'

He went on for some time explaining it all to her, and Lissa listened, making only an occasional comment or asking a question. She knew that Hugo was thinking aloud more than talking to her. She didn't mind. If just by being there she was helping him, she was happy.

At last he said, 'I must be boring you to shreds.'

'Not at all. I'm very interested.' She added a trifle wryly, 'We don't get doctors offering lengthy explanations all that often.'

'No, I suppose not.' He smiled apologetically, then rose and said, 'Would you like some more coffee?'

'No, thanks.' Lissa stood up. 'It's late, Hugo. I really must be going.' In the glow of the mushroom lights surrounding the pool he looked larger than life, and she felt a dangerous trembling start up inside her.

'I'll drive you home now,' he said, in a voice that suggested a spring tightly coiled.

For a moment neither moved, as though neither wanted to be first to make the move that would end the evening. Then abruptly both moved at once and collided. Lissa felt Hugo's arms steady her, but they did not fall away, they tightened around her, and she was looking up into his face and seeing the hunger there, and the deliberate restraint. Her heart ached with her own longing, and love overwhelmed her. She should have gone hours ago, she knew. By staying she had minute by minute increased her vulnerability. The magnetic field between them was too strong to resist.

She ceased to try. She knew, as Hugo's hands strayed wildly into her hair and his mouth covered hers, that she was powerless to order events, and strangely the knowledge did not panic her, it made her feel comforted. There would be no more fighting her feelings. Tonight she would give them full rein, and give Hugo the full measure of her love. He needed physical renewal, and she could give it to him. Wasn't that what love was all about? Helping the person you loved no matter what the cost to yourself?

Hugo seemed to sense her change of mood, the capitulation that was in every fibre of her as she responded to his kiss. He did not speak, but groaned once softly against her neck, then, as though to relieve her of responsibility for her actions, he picked her up and carried her into the house.

Lissa was self-consciously aware of being carried into a large bedroom with a large bed. She was aware of warm tones of brown and ochre with touches of green, and a soft creamy carpet beneath her bare feet as Hugo set her down. There was a silk-shaded lamp, half-drawn curtains, and then cool creamy sheets under her naked body, her hair spread out on the pillow. Her clothes were on the floor where Hugo had flung them along with his own. He had paused only for a moment, looking at her, tenderly stroking her from her shoulders to her hips, pressing his lips to her breasts, murmuring, 'You're beautiful. . .'

And she had heard herself saying, without feeling in the least foolish, 'You're beautiful too.'

He lay beside her for a moment. 'Are you sure?' he asked softly, toying with strands of her hair.

'There has to be a first time,' she murmured, holding out her arms to him, and folding them tightly around the taut warm body that covered hers. The lamp went out, but Lissa could still see his face quite clearly in the moonlight that streamed through the gap in the curtains. But she didn't need to see, she only needed to feel, to lose herself totally in the avalanche of emotion that swept over her, startling her, amazing her, changing her so that never again would she be quite the same.

She woke to find sunlight slanting through the window and was vaguely aware of pleasant dreams evaporating. For a moment she thought she was in her own bed at the flat, but as sleep fell away a tide of warm remembrance engulfed her. She found Hugo's arms still around her, and turned to snuggle closer. He stirred, opened his eyes and looked at her, at first with faint surprise, then a swift shadow of concern.

'Are you all right?'

'I'm fine.'

He propped himself on his elbow and looked at her. 'Lovely. . .' A smile started. 'Who seduced whom, I wonder?'

'Oh, I decided it was time I took the plunge.' Why she felt an urge to be flippant, Lissa didn't know. Perhaps it was embarrassment at finding herself naked in his bed in broad daylight. Yet there had been no embarrassment last night, and she had no regrets this morning. Not yet, anyway.

His scrutiny was intent. 'I didn't hurt you?'

'Of course not. It was wonderful, Hugo. You're a very good teacher.' Warm colour flooded her cheeks, and the blush made him chuckle.

He bent to kiss her. 'You make love better than you play golf! I can't believe you haven't had a lot of practice.'

'I don't think you have to.' Her blush deepened. 'Is it so terrible to be twenty-four and still a virgin?'

'A little unusual perhaps, but not terrible.' He looked at her with a tenderness she had not expected to see. 'I'm more than a little flattered. Thank you for staying last night, Lissa. You don't know how much it meant to me.'

Was that all he was going to say—*thank you*? Lissa felt her eyes misting over, but struggled to restrain the tears. 'I had a good time too,' she said, mustering a smile. 'But I think I'd better get up and go home. Maggie will be back and wondering where I've been all night, and I'm on duty this morning.'

'I think you're going to be a little late,' Hugo said huskily against her ear as he pinned her to the bed with purposeful strength. 'You'd better start thinking up an excuse, because I want to make love to you again.'

Lissa hadn't the will to argue. She would never argue with Hugo again, she thought. But there was no time then for thinking up excuses for being late. She folded her arms tightly around him and felt the tension in him as passion rapidly mounted again and found its response in her own welcoming body. As the crescendo approached, from the back of her mind there suddenly surfaced the incantation she had thought firmly put down. . .let him love me. . .let him love me. . .

CHAPTER SEVEN

WHEN Lissa let herself into the flat, Maggie's door was closed tight, which meant she was presumably still fast asleep and unaware that Lissa had not returned last night. Lissa was greatly relieved that she did not have to invent an explanation as to where she'd spent the night. She was glad she hadn't wasted time having breakfast at Hugo's.

If Maggie woke before she left for work, she would only have to pretend she'd overslept. Maggie was a heavy sleeper, fortunately, so with a bit of luck, Lissa thought, she might be away again before Maggie stirred. As there was still no sign of her when she left, Lissa left a hastily scrawled note on the table hoping she'd had a good weekend and apologising for drinking all the orange juice.

In the end she was no more than half an hour late. For once a tram came along as she reached the stop, the traffic was light and the journey took less time than usual. Her excuse that she had overslept was accepted by Warren with a sly smile which Lissa ignored, trusting there was no blush on her cheeks.

'Had a good day off, did you?' he enquired, staring at her as though it showed.

'Not bad,' she answered. 'I started learning to play golf.' The minute she mentioned it, she saw the pitfalls.

Warren's eyebrow cocked curiously. He was a keen golfer himself. 'I thought you derided the game.'

An airy response was the only one that would hide

her feelings, so Lissa said, 'I did, but I've been persuaded that it does have its challenges.'

'Where did you play?'

Lissa swallowed. Warren might know where Hugo played and he was quite capable of putting two and two together. She managed a laugh that didn't sound too nervous. 'To tell you the truth, I'm not sure. A friend took me. It was in the eastern suburbs somewhere,' she said vaguely, searching desperately for a likely place in a totally different direction from the course they had played on. 'Waverley?'

Warren looked sceptical. 'That's where I play. I was there most of yesterday, but I didn't see you.' His look suggested that he wasn't at all sure she was being quite straight with him.

Of all the places to choose! Lissa was regretting the tangle she was getting herself into. 'Well, it was somewhere around there,' she said, and was grateful when one of the other nurses interrupted and Warren went off to see a patient.

Lissa firmly told herself that while she was on duty she must not let herself be distracted by what had happened yesterday. She must put it right out of her mind until this evening. Then she would set about rationalising it. However, it was impossible to dismiss, even temporarily, such a milestone in her life. Although she managed to push it all to the back of her mind while she worked through her regular tasks and dealt with the needs and problems of her small patients, while she was taking her coffee-break everything came flooding back.

For once she was alone in the nurses' room for a few minutes, and as she stood by the window gazing across to the city skyline, her thoughts flowed uninterrupted.

Uppermost in her mind was the question—where do we go from here? There had been no time this morning for talk. Hugo had been in a rush too. Even in the car when he drove her home, he had said little, and nothing at all about last night.

Lissa was still in a state of shock. For her last night had been momentous, but what about Hugo? For him it had been important, but in a different way. How did he feel now? she wondered. Would he want to continue the affair? And if so, did she? What would the future hold if she did?

She stared out of the window in an agony of indecision. Common sense told her that having an affair with Hugo was about the most destructive thing she could do to herself. But if he wanted her, could she refuse him? Could she deny herself the kind of ecstasy she had enjoyed in his arms last night? She was glad Hugo had been the first. Because she loved him, she had given him her heart and soul, and she had no complaints about what she had received in return. She loved him more now, not less.

It couldn't have been just a physical thing on his part, she told herself, wrapped around with remembered warmth and tenderness. He had made it very clear that he enjoyed her company, liked talking to her. She wasn't so dumb she couldn't talk about his research. If they were together often, then surely. . .surely in time he would come to care for her as she cared for him?

Or was she being foolish and indulging in wishful thinking again? He told you not to take him too seriously, she reminded herself, but last night's loving seemed to cancel out that caution.

She rinsed her coffee-mug and determinedly pushed

her personal dilemma into the background. Maybe when she had seen Hugo again things would be clearer. As she pulled open the door, she heard his name, and her stomach lurched.

'Good morning, Hugo.' It was Jayne Rossney who breezily addressed him.

Lissa shrank back. They were only a few feet away, standing in the corridor where they could not see her, but she could hear their conversation clearly. Somehow she could not bring herself to go out, speak normally to Hugo, and continue on to the ward. She was afraid that Jayne would be able to guess from her face what had happened.

'Did you have a good weekend?' Jayne asked.

'Yes, I did.' To Lissa's ears Hugo's voice had a new timbre. The sound of it struck deeply into her very being now.

'Sunday was such a perfect day,' Jayne went on in a complaining tone, 'and there was I standing in for Geoffrey Walker whose wife decided to have her baby three weeks prematurely when I could have been playing golf with you. I'll never perfect my swing if I don't get in more practice.'

Lissa's fingers were clenched so tightly in her palms, the pain was shooting up her arms. She was hurting deep inside too. She backed away from the door. She couldn't bear to hear any more. What she had heard was quite clear enough. Hugo had been going to play golf with Jayne Rossney, but she'd had to cancel. So he had asked Lissa instead. Maybe last night had been nothing to do with her personally at all. Maybe if Jayne had been with him yesterday, she would have ended up in his bed last night. And taken on balance, Jayne was surely the companion he would have preferred.

The chances were, Lissa thought, that Hugo would now avoid her. She had served her purpose. And, as her father had warned her not to, she had made an even bigger fool of herself.

The bleakness that descended was almost over-whelming, but she went back to work determined not to behave as though it were the end of the world. She had known all along that Hugo was never going to develop any real interest in her. She had already behaved foolishly in coming back to Australia, so she must take the consequences. It wasn't Hugo's fault. He'd promised her nothing. She vowed not to show him any sign that she had hoped for more than was reasonable. She was, she told herself, going to be *adult* about it. She was no longer going to harbour vain hopes, and she was never going to indulge in stupid nonsense like willing him to fall in love with her. She had got what she deserved for dabbling in such super-stitious rubbish.

Feeling strong and sensible and very much together again, Lissa worked her shift in her usual efficient way. She kept her eyes firmly averted when doors opened and closed, never once looking up to see if Hugo was there. She shut her ears to the sound of telephones ringing and refused to hope when she was obliged to answer one.

'Are you all right, Lissa?' Karyn asked suddenly while they were dispensing the afternoon's medi-cations. 'You look very intense today.'

Lissa had been sure she looked her normal relaxed self. 'I'm fine,' she answered. 'A bit tired, I suppose.'

'Late night last night?' Karyn enquired with a grin.

Lissa refused to feel pain. 'Yes, it was rather.'

'You haven't had a row with Paul, have you?' asked Karyn with sympathy.

'I didn't see Paul this weekend,' Lissa said, sounding more terse than she intended because there was a stupid lump in her throat and a prickling behind her eyes.

Karyn did not probe, and Lissa attempted to make light-hearted conversation that wasn't personal. But it was hard, so hard. Emotions were not that easily reined in. It wasn't easy to maintain a matter-of-fact, cheerful front when deep down you were hurting. Falling in love was so easy, she thought wistfully, but falling out of love was so hard.

If Lissa nurtured any lingering hope that Hugo would want to regard Sunday as the beginning of a relationship, it had faded by the end of the week. She had seen him twice, but always with other people around. She had avoided his eyes, and had carried out whatever professional duties he asked her to promptly and efficiently. Despite her effort to avoid it, she had on one of those occasions found herself briefly alone with him.

He had turned to her at once and murmured, 'Are you angry with me?'

She had widened her eyes innocently. 'Angry? Why should I be?'

'You don't feel badly about what happened on Sunday?' The dark eyes were anxious, probing.

Her heart was thumping, making her feel breathless. 'Hugo, I really don't think there's any need to discuss it,' she said. 'What happened happened. I guess we both benefited.'

She tightened her grip on the examination trolley she was returning to the treatment-room. He slid a hand over hers. 'Lissa. . . I don't want you to take this personally, but there's no point in continuing. . .you do see that, don't you?'

'Of course I do, Hugo. I never expected—anything to come of it. I understand.'

His mouth had a tenderness that made her yearn to kiss him right there and then, regardless of observers. But she didn't, and he said, 'I wouldn't want you to be hurt.'

'If I'm not involved, I can't be,' Lissa lied. She gave the trolley a shove and he withdrew his hand from hers. If he had intended to say any more, the opportunity was lost, because Jayne Rossney appeared.

'Ah, Hugo, you're still here. Sorry I couldn't get here for your round. Can you spare a minute now?' she asked, eyes slicing Lissa into small pieces. 'I'd like to discuss the baby with hiatus hernia. When are we going to operate?' She was drawing him away, back to the ward, and he was going oh, so willingly, Lissa thought, as she shoved the trolley through the door with more force than was necessary. Well, at least he'd had the grace to tell her. And the decency not to lead her on. It still hurt, though, knowing that her part in unlocking his emotions would be to the advantage of Jayne Rossney, or if not her then someone like her.

Lissa had almost finished stripping the trolley and putting the instruments in the autoclave when Paul walked in.

'Hello, my lissom lovely,' he greeted her. 'Are you going off with your secret lover again this weekend, or are you coming windsurfing with me?'

'I haven't got a secret lover,' she responded a little testily.

He inclined his head quizzically. 'No? Then what's

the matter with you lately, sweetheart? You're as jumpy as a cricket and as tensed up as an overwound clock. If you ask Dr Norris, which you never do, your love life is suddenly in turmoil.' He put his fingers under her chin and tilted it. His hazel eyes were teasing as always. 'Why you can't fall for a nice uncomplicated guy like me I don't know.'

I don't know either, Lissa thought, angry with herself. 'Because I know you don't really want me to,' she said.

He was half serious when he said, 'I might be changing my mind. We've got a lot going for us. . .'

'Please, Paul, don't!' Lissa's voice cracked.

He clasped her in his arms. 'Methinks the lady needs a shoulder to cry on.'

She felt too weak to resist. Wearily she let her head rest on his shoulder. She didn't sob her heart out, even though she felt like doing so, but Paul's cheerful comforting released her tension. It was Jayne Rossney's slightly sarcastic tones which interrupted eventually.

'You two do find each other irresistible, don't you?' she said, coming in. 'It's a wonder any nursing gets done around here. You ought to be ashamed, Paul, chatting up the girls while they're on duty.' She laughed gaily. 'Do you have a woman in every ward?' The look she gave Lissa was pitying, and calculated to sting.

'You're a bitch, Jayne,' said Paul, and although he was smiling, Lissa could tell from his eyes he was angry with her. 'Just because you're having it off with the Chief, you think you can talk smart to everyone.'

Lissa stepped back, shocked by Paul's uncharacteristically abrasive manner. Jayne too looked taken aback.

'I was only joking,' she said, smiling sweetly at Lissa. 'I'm sure Lissa doesn't believe me.' She did not, however, Lissa noticed, deny Paul's remark about Hugo. She went on, 'I was looking for Warren and obviously he's not here. Any idea where I'll find him, Lissa?'

'He went to Radiology with a patient,' Lissa said stiffly, her dislike of Dr Rossney undiminished.

Jayne swept out, and Paul slammed a fist into his palm. 'I'd like to put her over my knee!'

Light dawned on Lissa. 'Oh, Paul. . .not over your knee! In your arms, surely?'

He gave a quirky grin. 'More fool me, eh?' He raked a hand through his unruly red hair. 'I guess I need psychiatry!'

'She's a beautiful woman.'

'And I'm no oil painting. Girls like her go for blokes like Hugo Stanfield—guys with the good looks and the status.'

Lissa gave him a warm hug. 'Paul, you're much too nice, much too good for a woman like Jayne.' She drew back. Like Hugo. Why did men so often fall for the pretty face and seem unconcerned about the character behind it?

Paul said ruefully, 'Well, are we going to console each other this weekend?'

Lissa smiled. 'Of course. I'm off on Sunday again.'

It was several weeks before Lissa had a full weekend off, and with that prospect came a dilemma. Jacqui Darling had rung to say they would be living in the hospital flat for a few weeks while their house was being redecorated, but had insisted that Lissa must nevertheless come up to Maneroo for her next two-day break.

'We haven't seen you since you came back,' she said reproachfully. 'You must promise, Lissa. The house will be finished by then.'

Lissa didn't mention Hugo, or that she had promised him that she would arrange a balloon trip for him. In the circumstances it seemed rather pointless to take it any further.

Their paths had crossed regularly as they had always done and they had talked about the patients in the normal way. They had even exchanged pleasantries about the weather, opinions about canteen food, and staff shortages. Lissa was sure that her feelings were well under control and that no one, least of all Hugo, could possibly guess how she felt about him. They had even riled each other in a minor way a couple of times.

Therefore the thing to do was to ignore the ballooning promise. Hugo had probably forgotten all about it anyway, and even if she did bring it up, he was hardly likely to want to take her up on it. He had plenty of other things to occupy him, including, Lissa supposed, the beautiful but rather bitchy Dr Rossney.

He had changed, she thought, since that Sunday they had spent together. He did not look so shut-in lately. His manner was more relaxed, and there was a subtle difference in the way he spoke, his tone less brusque. But, because her eye was now attuned to it, she noticed that he still maintained a certain almost imperceptible reserve where the children were concerned. It was as though the doctor who attended them and the man under the white coat were two separate people. He had broken through one barrier, but perhaps he never would come to terms with his past. Or was Jayne

Rossney the woman who would help him over that hurdle? Lissa forced herself to acknowledge that, alone with Hugo, Jayne was probably a very different person.

So she said nothing about the ballooning. She was afraid that if she did, he would think she was trying to resurrect something between them. It was therefore an immense surprise when one day he asked casually, 'Have you been ballooning lately?'

She was in Warren's office alone searching for some old case notes to send on to a patient's GP when he appeared.

'Not lately. I'm going up to Maneroo the weekend after next. I may have a chance then.'

His dark eyes were steady, unrevealing. 'Any chance I could join you? You did offer. . .'

Lissa felt her heart flip. He wasn't serious, surely? 'You still want to try it?'

'Sure.' His eyes were steady, giving nothing away. 'You wouldn't mind?'

'Not at all. You're very welcome to come,' Lissa said. 'I'll phone Jacqui and tell her.'

'I hope I won't be putting them out.'

'They'll love to have you,' she assured him. 'Jacqui suggested I fly up on Friday to Hindmarsh and she'll meet me.'

'That's fine by me,' he agreed.

That night Lissa rang Jacqui to ask if she could bring Hugo.

'Of course you can bring Hugo.' Jacqui's voice crackled with curiosity. 'Single rooms or double?' She chuckled.

'Single, of course!'

'I see. You're just good friends.'

'Not even that really. He's our consultant—doing research into SIDS.'

'No time for attractive women?' Jacqui teased.

Lissa maintained her offhandedness. 'If anything, he has designs on a doctor at the SCG. His interest in me is purely as an arranger of a balloon trip.' She added a few details about Hugo's work and finished, 'You'll like him, Jacqui.'

'*You* sound like an admirer,' Jacqui commented. She chuckled again. 'For a while I thought David had designs on another female, but he didn't. Maybe Hugo will prove to be as devious!'

'I don't think so.'

It would be hard, Lissa knew, to keep her real feelings about Hugo concealed from Jacqui. They had shared a flat for long enough to know each other very well, and Jacqui was a very perceptive person.

A couple of days before the proposed weekend at Maneroo, Jacqui rang, very upset.

'Lissa, this is awful, I know, but would you and Hugo mind very much staying at the motel?'

'Why? What's happened?'

'Nothing! I was positive the decorating would be finished by now, and it would have been if one of the fellows hadn't gone down with flu, then the other one caught it, and now everything's at a standstill. They're not anywhere near finished yet, and the whole place is in chaos. So, as it's rather cramped here, I've booked you both in at the Maneroo Motel, and it's on us, of course.'

'Wouldn't you rather we postponed it?' asked Lissa.

'Oh, no, love, don't do that,' Jacqui pleaded. 'I'm so looking forward to seeing you.'

She sounded so disappointed at the idea of a post-ponement that Lissa hadn't the heart to press it.

'Are you flying up?' Jacqui asked.

'Yes.'

'Good! That means we'll have more time together. Can you still manage Friday's commuter special?'

'I hope so.'

'Till Friday, then. I'll be there to meet you.'

Hugo picked Lissa up at home on Friday afternoon and drove to the airport.

'You got away on time,' he commented.

'Luckily, yes. It was quiet on the ward today, thank goodness. We've had a pretty hectic week.'

'And coped splendidly as always.' The compliment was matter-of-fact, and all the more warming for that. He had no need to flatter her.

Their conversation was sporadic, inconsequential and detached. They were not two people going away for a romantic weekend together, but two colleagues taking a trip because of a common interest. Lissa was able to sound detached, but underneath she was already finding it a strain being so close to Hugo. Memories of the night they had spent together kept sweeping across her mind. Just looking at his strong brown hands gripping the steering wheel churned her up inside. She was glad they were not driving all the way; several hours sitting beside him would have been hard to bear. It would be easier, she hoped, when they were with Jacqui and David. David and Hugo would be bound to talk shop, leaving her and Jacqui to gossip.

Both David and Jacqui were at the airport to meet them. While the two women hugged each other in glad reunion, Hugo hung back, until Lissa introduced him.

Lissa saw Jacqui's alert gaze sweep swiftly over him with approval. David welcomed him with a warm handshake, then announced that they were having dinner in Hindmarsh.

Jacqui linked arms with Lissa. 'It's so good to see you.' She glanced at her and whispered, 'But you're not as sparkly as usual. Anything the matter?'

'No. A bit tired, probably. We were all run off our feet this week.'

The two men were already chatting amicably as they walked ahead to David's car and stowed the luggage in it. 'I think Hugo's smashing,' said Jacqui, with a sly grin. 'Are you sure you're not being a dark horse, Lissa?'

Lissa shook her head, then, seeing Jacqui's sceptical glance, admitted part of the truth. 'It's a bit complicated, Jacqui. I'll tell you about it some time.'

'He's married?'

'No. It's a bit difficult to explain in a nutshell, but believe me, there's nothing between Hugo and me, nor is there likely to be.'

'But you'd like there to be?'

Lissa's voice was very low. 'Yes.'

'No chance at all?'

'None. Do you mind if we leave it there, Jacqui? I'll explain some time, I promise.'

They went to an Italian restaurant that was apparently a favourite of Jacqui and David's, and the talk was mainly about ballooning and babies. Jacqui was bubbling with good spirits because she was pregnant, and as she talked Lissa could not help glancing at Hugo and wondering how this kind of conversation affected him. It must be hard, seeing other people's happiness, knowing your own had been snatched tragically from you. He gave no sign, however. The man seemed to have an iron control.

Inevitably, the conversation touched on his work with SIDS research and Lissa marvelled again at the calm way he was able to talk about it, giving no hint of his personal tragedy. Was the past gradually receding? she wondered. Was he coming back into the real world wholly at last instead of partly? She hoped so, and was glad if she had contributed in some small way to his rehabilitation.

It was late when they arrived in Maneroo, but they accepted the Darlings' invitation to have a nightcap and stayed talking in the flat until midnight. Lissa was pleased at how well Hugo and David were getting along. Once or twice her eyes met Hugo's and she could not help remembering the feel of his smooth skin and springy chest hairs, the sensuousness of his mouth, and a sharp pang of jealousy at the thought of Jayne Rossney in his arms, in his bed, knifed her. He was hers for this weekend, but not the way she really wanted him.

David drove them to the motel and waited while they registered and were given their keys, then he said goodnight and promised to call for them early. If the weather was suitable, Hugo was to have a balloon trip on both Saturday and Sunday mornings.

Their motel units were next door to each other. Lissa slid her key in the door of hers. 'Goodnight, Hugo,' she said. Her imagination suddenly ran riot. Suppose he took her in his arms now?

But he didn't. 'Tired?' he asked.

'A bit.'

'Do you want me to call you?'

'I have a travelling alarm clock. Do you want me to call *you*?'

'No, I'll be awake. Goodnight, Lissa. Sleep tight.'

Amazingly enough, she did. The tiring week had drained her energy, and despite her emotional turmoil, she was asleep almost as soon as her head touched the pillow. The alarm woke her from a deep sleep and she lay for a few moments after she had shut it off, coming to as though from an anaesthetic. Then she got up and showered and dressed, and was ready by the time David and Jacqui tooted outside.

Hugo was already there talking to David as she pulled her door closed and crossed the forecourt to join them. There was a bit of a breeze, but David said it wasn't strong enough to ground them. The sun was just coming up and dazzled their eyes as they drove out to the launching site. Travelling the bush road through the wide acres of wheat and grazing land, with its limitless horizons, Lissa felt a thrill of something primitive. City girl that she was, she had nevertheless discovered a communion with the wide open spaces that she'd never thought possible. She understood how Jacqui felt. This country, she thought, has a unique beauty that hooks you. I *am* glad I came back.

She was in the back with Hugo, who remarked, 'I suppose the balloon flights are very popular.'

David said, 'There was a falling off for a while after a couple of freak accidents, but people realise the risks are minimal. Accidents can always happen, but really ballooning is one of the safest forms of aeronautics.'

'You have to take some risks in life,' said Jacqui. 'I was terrified the first time I went up, but I didn't let David see it. I'm glad I didn't chicken out, because it's a glorious experience, isn't it, Lissa?'

'Fabulous,' Lissa agreed. She glanced at Hugo and caught a strange expression on his face, as though for a moment he was caught up in some internal conflict. She didn't think it was fear of flying.

It was nearly an hour before they could take their trip. Hugo showed immense interest in the balloons and was eager to assist with the launching of them. He's not in the least afraid, Lissa thought. She was still a little nervous even though she had been up before, but it was only the same kind of nervousness she felt when she boarded a jet to fly somewhere.

At last it was their turn. Jacqui had decided not to go with them.

'I'm just a little queasy still at this hour of the morning,' she confessed to Lissa. 'And Dr Darling says no flying!'

Lissa climbed into the basket with the two men, put on the cap provided and held on tightly to the suede-padded edge of the gondola. Hugo was examining the functioning of the gas jets which inflated the balloon.

David gave the nod to a helper who unhitched the rope attached to the bumper bar of a four-wheel drive, and slowly the basket began to rise. The great nylon envelope of the balloon soared above their heads, its garish colours iridescent in the sunlight. The slight breeze rocked the basket as they rose, but the higher they went the smoother became the flight.

Hugo finally looked across at Lissa and smiled. 'Pretty good, eh?'

'Fantastic,' she agreed.

David began to point out landmarks. They were aloft for half an hour, and finally came down in a paddock not far from a dam, where the retrieval vehicle reached them a few minutes later.

'We were lucky,' said David. 'The wind's getting up and we'll be grounded now. No more trips this morning. The rules are very strict.'

'Did you enjoy it?' Lissa asked Hugo. 'Was it as good as you expected?' Her cheeks were flushed with the sharpness of the air aloft and her exhilaration.

'It was remarkable,' he said. 'Quite a heady experience.'

'And you weren't even nervous,' she teased. He was taking it very much in his stride, with his usual calm in any situation, but she felt that he had been as exhilarated as she.

His dark eyes were slightly hooded. 'Some risks are easier to take than others,' he said cryptically.

Hugo insisted on treating them to breakfast at a hotel, then Jacqui suggested a picnic.

'You can't say no,' she said, 'because it's all prepared and the baskets are in the boot of the car.' There were lots of wonderful places to visit, she enthused—the Big Desert, the Little Desert, or the Grampians range, and there were numerous lakes in the area. When Hugo expressed an interest in birdlife, they settled on a long run into South Australia to Bool Lagoon, which neither Jacqui or David had visited.

It was a leisurely day spent walking, birdwatching and talking. The four of them got along well, and Lissa was pleased that Hugo seemed to be relaxed and enjoying himself. Every minute he seemed to be unbending more, and when she heard him laugh it sent shivers down her spine. She avoided sticking close to him in case he misinterpreted it, but that wasn't hard to do as he seemed engrossed most of the time in talking to David. Only once did they touch, and that was on a walk when he offered his hand to help her over a dry gully. She leapt agilely enough, but her momentum caused her to bump against him and for a moment his arm went around her to steady her.

'OK?'

'Fine.' She was breathless, and to cover the sudden flushing of her skin that his proximity had caused, she hurried on to catch up with Jacqui, now some distance ahead.

'I do like your Hugo,' Jacqui said later when she and Lissa were packing up the picnic baskets while the men wandered off spotting ducks on the lagoons. 'And the way he looks at you sometimes, I'd swear there's nothing platonic in his mind! Are you sure there's no chance. . .?'

'It would take a miracle,' Lissa sighed.

'You're in love with him, aren't you?'

It was no use pretending. 'Yes.' Lissa closed her eyes for a moment against the sudden welling of tears. She shook her head. 'I'd rather not talk about it, Jacqui. It's been a terrific day. I know Hugo's enjoyed it. I haven't often seen him so relaxed.'

Their conversation lapsed as the men returned. It was time to go. There was little conversation on the long drive back to Maneroo. Hugo offered to drive, and David agreed. The two men sat in front while Jacqui and Lissa occupied the back seat. They did not talk much, however, because Jacqui dozed off. Lissa watched the landscape flashing past, listened to snatches of the conversation from the front seat, and finally felt her eyelids drooping too.

After the big picnic lunch, none of them was hungry, so Jacqui suggested a light tea at the hospital flat. And after it, when he caught Lissa yawning, Hugo insisted on an early night.

'Jacqui's half asleep too,' he said. 'And if we're to be up at the crack of dawn again tomorrow. . .' He glanced at David questioningly.

'Same time,' said David, adding, 'If you're still keen.'

'You bet! I could get addicted,' Hugo admitted.

David drove them back to the motel and left them at the entrance. When Lissa couldn't stifle a yawn once more, Hugo chuckled and put his arm around her shoulders. 'Great day.'

'Terrific,' she agreed.

'I like your friends.'

'They like you too. I'm so glad you and David hit it off so well.'

'He's a nice guy. And his wife's a charmer.'

'Yes. . .'

They had paused outside their units. Lissa inserted her key in the lock and turned it. 'Goodnight, Hugo. See you in the morning.' She pushed the door open and went in.

'Lissa. . .'

She turned round. One moment he was silhouetted against the stars, the next she was in his arms and the door had slammed shut. His mouth was on hers hungrily, his arms holding her so tightly she gasped.

'Lissa, I want you like crazy,' he was muttering wildly. 'All day I've been aching to touch you. . .'

The forecourt lights dimly illuminated the room. Lissa did not resist as he pushed her backwards to the bed, and she fell with him on to it. His hands were warm and arousing on the bare skin beneath her top as they pushed aside the flimsy bra and caressed her breasts. Then his palm was circling the flat plane of her stomach, and exploring the sensitive grooves of her thighs. His passionate hunger fired her own needs and for long moments they writhed together in a kind of mad frenzy, encumbered by clothing but unable to release each other for long enough to shed it.

At last Lissa heard herself whispering, 'Love me, Hugo. . .please love me. . .'

Her words had an extraordinary effect. He raised himself abruptly and sat on the edge of the bed, his face in his hands, ignoring her.

Lissa reached for the bedside lamp. Its dull sheen was an intrusion, but she left it on. 'Hugo, what's wrong?' His shoulders were shaking, and when she touched him he flung his hands down and faced her, distraught.

'Lissa, I'm sorry, sorry, sorry. . .' He held her hands in a vice grip. 'I shouldn't have come in. I told myself I wouldn't, but I couldn't help it.' He looked at her steadily for a moment. 'It's no good, Lissa. I can't ever go through that nightmare again.' He touched her face tenderly. 'I mustn't fall in love with you and I don't want you to fall in love with me. There's no future in it, Lissa. I'll never be a normal husband and father again. . .'

'Yes, you will,' she said softly, bringing her mouth close to his, rubbing her lips against his. 'It's just a matter of time.'

'Five years already,' he said bitterly. 'How can I ask anyone to wait?'

Lissa took a deep breath. 'Hugo—I'd wait.'

He didn't seem surprised. He drew her head against his chest and nuzzled her hair. 'That's what you say now. But I don't know how long, Lissa, I don't know if ever. . .if ever I could bring myself to father another child.' He raised her face to his. 'I could easily fall in love with you, Lissa, but it's better that I don't. Better for both of us. I should have known that coming away with you this weekend would have been a temptation. I'm not going to be guilty of using you, Lissa—I have too much respect for you to do that. A barren affair is not what you want. You want a nice normal marriage to a nice normal man with no hang-ups.'

'I want to marry *you*,' Lissa whispered, not caring now that he knew.

He held her close again. 'That's what you say now, Lissa,' he said again. 'But I've endured one marriage's destruction, and I'm not going to risk tearing apart another. You're young and healthy and normal. You want children, the kind of happy, stable family life you're accustomed to. If you were to marry a man who can't bear to be a father again, it would eventually end in bitterness.'

'But you won't always be this way,' Lissa said pleadingly.

'I think I will be,' he said slowly, 'at least until I know how to prevent babies dying in their cots for no apparent reason.'

It was the ultimate argument, and Lissa had no answer to it. 'There may never be a definitive answer,' she said, looking away from him, defeated.

Painfully, he replied, 'I know.'

His acceptance suddenly angered her, and she lifted her face and with a surge of fighting spirit, said, 'You can't keep running away from it, Hugo. You're destroying yourself. It's a million to one chance it would ever happen to a child of yours again.'

'I know, but. . .' He moved restlessly away from the bed, then turned, saying roughly, 'I thought you understood.'

'I do understand. I try to. . . I know what you're going through. . .'

'I don't need your pity,' he flung at her.

'Wanting to help you isn't pity!'

'You think marrying you would help me?' he asked in a tone so scathing, Lissa flinched. 'That's very self-sacrificial of you, Lissa, but what if it failed?'

'That's a risk we'd both have to take.'

He became hard and scornful. 'What would you do, Lissa? Would you stay or go? How long would it be before your patience ran out? Right now you're full of missionary zeal, but when you finally realised you really were shackled to an emotional cripple. . .'

'You're a doctor, Hugo,' Lissa burst out. 'You of all people shouldn't talk this way.'

'I'm a human being,' he flashed back. 'Doctors aren't immune from human frailties—you told me so yourself.'

'And I wouldn't blame you for it. I wouldn't care if we never had children,' she said.

He looked at her with scepticism. 'So you say now, but one day you might regret it, and even if you didn't I should still feel guilty because I was depriving you. That's when the disintegration would begin.' His expression did not soften, but he laid a hand on her shoulder and said, 'You're a brave girl, Lissa, but a foolish one. You're a little starry-eyed because I was your first lover. I wish now. . .' He removed his hand abruptly. 'I'm not going to let you do something you may regret.'

Lissa knew it was useless to argue with him. 'Please go,' she said, looking at the floor. 'Please go, Hugo.'

He touched the top of her head briefly. 'I'm sorry, Lissa.'

CHAPTER EIGHT

During the weeks following the weekend at Maneroo, Lissa often said to herself, What am I doing here? Why don't I just pack it in?

But somehow she couldn't. She had her pride, after all. She had cut and run once before, then come back. This time she intended to stay put and work things out on the spot. If there was even now a tiny spark of hope that if she was patient Hugo might change, she was careful not to acknowledge it. If sometimes, after he had been in the wards, her wayward mind whispered, *make him change his mind*, she refused to acknowledge that too. She knew she must face the fact that although Hugo might be attracted to her physically, might even think it possible to fall in love with her, he was unlikely to marry her even if he did overcome his inhibitions.

At least he had been honest with her. He had shown consideration for her feelings that many men would not have done. He didn't believe she loved him. He thought it was only pity she felt, or that she wanted to be in love with him because he was the first man to make love to her. So he could easily have used her. He could even have led her to believe that their relationship had a future, but he hadn't done that. He had distanced himself for her sake. That night in Maneroo nothing she could have said would have convinced him that to her nothing else in her life would ever be as important as simply being with him. She had had to accept his decision. She had had no choice. Hugo's marriage had not survived the trauma of his daughter's loss, so she could hardly blame him for caution. If he had loved her perhaps it would have been different, but obviously he didn't.

If she had cut and run now, she knew, Hugo would have felt some responsibility and remorse, so it was partly to save him that that she stayed. And there was, of course, her promotion. She was pleased to have it confirmed, yet her feelings were mixed. Becoming charge nurse brought her new responsibilities, but also more contact with Hugo. And with Jayne Rossney, whose dislike of her seemed to deepen with the announcement of Lissa's new role.

At Warren's farewell party, which was held in the hospital's lecture hall and was attended by a good proportion of the staff, who came and went in relays throughout the evening, Lissa avoided Hugo. She danced mostly with Paul, whom she still saw quite a lot of when they were off duty, and who posed no emotional problems. She knew his eyes followed Jayne Rossney, but that didn't worry her. It occurred to her now and then that she and Paul might eventually become so accustomed to each other's company that they would drift into marriage even if they weren't in love. She was fond of the young doctor and they would probably make a good steady marriage, if not an exciting one. Maybe marriages like that were preferable. But while Jayne Rossney was unmarried, Lissa knew that Paul would remain besotted by her. The condescending way Jayne treated him often made Lissa angry and did nothing to enhance her opinion of the young doctor.

Lissa was off duty, so she was able to spend the

whole evening at Warren's party. She made a determined effort to enjoy herself. It was her party too in a
way, since everyone was congratulating her on taking
over from Warren. She had just come out of an
energetic old-fashioned waltz with Warren and was
standing on the sidelines, breathless and slightly flushed
from the dance while he fetched her a drink, when
Hugo approached carrying two glasses. He looked
handsome in a soft grey suit with a dusty pink shirt and
toning tie.

'Warren asked me to bring your drink,' he said. 'He
had to take a phone call.'

'Thank you.' His fingertips brushed her hand as he
transferred the glass, and she quivered as she always
did when she accidentally touched him. It sometimes
happened in the ward, and she hadn't yet schooled
herself to be matter-of-fact about it.

His eyes travelled admiringly over her apple-green
dress with its swirly skirt and moulded bodice with
narrow shoulder-straps. Her skin was still smoothly
golden from the summer and her hair was loose, falling
in shining waves about her shoulders.

'You look a picture of health and vitality,' Hugo
said, teasing just a little.

'Fit as a fiddle,' she responded. 'Although that waltz
with Warren was an eye-opener. He's nearly twice my
age, but has twice my energy! Must be all that golf.'

'It's good for shoulder-muscles,' Hugo agreed. 'As
I'm sure you realised from your first acquaintance with
the game. Have you played since?'

Lissa wished she hadn't mentioned golf. 'No. I think
I can do without big shoulder-muscles,' she said flippantly. She sipped her drink. 'Mmm, this is nice.

Cafeteria Cocktail, I think they call it. I wonder what's in it.'

'The guys from Pharmacy brewed it, I'm told.'

Lissa pretended to gag. 'Help! We'll probably all have the DTs by morning!'

Hugo's eyes were intently on her, and that tantalising half smile was hovering around his lips. 'You should wear that colour often,' he told her. 'It suits you.'

'Thanks. You look pretty suave in grey!'

'Enough to qualify me for a dance?'

I can do it, Lissa thought. I'm strong. I can dance with this man I love, and enjoy it. I can accept a relationship on this level and, by not hankering for more, gain from it. 'Of course,' she said, finishing her drink and abandoning her glass to a nearby table.

'Your friend Paul won't mind?'

'My friend Paul is on call, and his bleeper went half an hour ago. I haven't seen him since.' Whatever was in the Cafeteria Cocktail, Lissa thought, it promoted bravado, nonchalance and a slightly devil-may-care attitude. But she wasn't quite brave enough to say, 'What about your friend Jayne?'

As luck would have it, the music changed tempo, the lights dimmed and the floor became quickly crowded so that movement was slow. Lissa let herself relax in Hugo's arms. Pretend, she told herself. Pretend this is all for real.

'Congratulations again on your promotion,' Hugo murmured.

'Thanks,' she said to his lapel.

His hand on the small of her back kept her close and his cheek brushed her hair, sending tremors through her and threatening her already fragile composure. Gradually his hand rose towards her shoulder-blade, a sensuous stroking that set her nerve-ends tingling.

'You're thinner,' he accused suddenly. 'I can feel your ribs.'

'I always lose weight in summer—it's the extra exercise. I get lazy in winter, and tempted by goodies. Don't worry, I'll be moon-faced again by August.'

He laughed, a low chuckle that reverberated in his chest. Lissa dared to glance up through lowered lashes and caught a smouldering look a moment before his lips brushed hers. The chemistry was still potent and they both knew it. Hugo gave an almost inaudible sigh, and Lissa let her head rest resignedly against his shoulder.

It wasn't until some time later that she realised someone had been watching them. The someone was Jayne Rossney. After the dance with Hugo, supper was announced, and Hugo gallantly offered to fill a plate for Lissa. While he was joining the crush at the tables at the far end of the hall, Lissa slipped out to the Ladies.

She was combing her hair when Jayne walked in. Unfortunately there were only the two of them there.

'You managed to get away for a while?' Lissa asked pleasantly, knowing the doctor had been on duty earlier.

Jayne, glamorous in black and silver with spangles in her upswept hair, looked very sophisticated. But her mood seemed as black as her dress. She gave Lissa a look of contempt.

'In time to see you smarming all over Hugo. Really, Lissa, have you no shame? Snuggling up to him in full view of everyone! I suppose you think your new job gives you the right to try and seduce a consultant.'

Lissa was more taken aback by the venom behind them than the actual words. 'Hugo asked me to dance,' she said. 'If I was close to him, it was because he was holding me close. Some people dance like that, Jayne. There's no need to be jealous.'

Jayne gave a burst of laughter. 'I'm not jealous! Good grief, I've no need to be that! It just disgusts me seeing cow-eyed nurses making up to him and embarrassing him like that. Poor Hugo, he's so courteous.'

Lissa stuffed her comb back in her bag. 'I got the impression he was enjoying himself, and not at all embarrassed.'

Jayne's mouth twisted a little. 'I think promotion must have gone to your head, Sister. But you nurses are all ambitious little harpies, aren't you? Maybe, since you can't take a hint, we'd better get it straight. Hugo is mine and has been for some considerable time.' Her eyes glittered possessively.

Lissa swallowed hard. It was easy to believe her. She looked Jayne over without rancour. She was beautiful, no doubt about that. She was also a year or two older than Lissa, but even to Lissa's mind less mature. Insecure, Warren had said. How was she with Hugo? Lissa wondered. Was she sympathetic? Was she a different person in Hugo's arms?

Someone came in and Lissa took the opportunity to escape. She felt awkward now going back to Hugo, who was balancing food and drink and looking around for her.

'I thought you'd run out on me,' he said, with a look that banished Jayne from her mind for an instant.

'I went to the Ladies,' she explained, adding, 'Jayne's here.'

'Is she?' His diffidence must be calculated, Lissa decided, because he did not want to acknowledge the intimacy between them.

As Lissa had expected, Jayne spotted them and marched over. She greeted Hugo, glanced at their plates as though suspecting that he had given her supper to Lissa, then stalked off to get some food for herself. At least she didn't have the gall to ask him to get it for her. When she came back she conducted a conversation with Hugo that deliberately excluded Lissa. Lissa would have left them to it, but that might have betrayed her feelings. She would escape, though, as soon as she had finished eating.

'Oh, isn't it wonderful to have a break from the kids at last!' Jayne exclaimed. 'Children can be so draining.' She flicked a glance at Lissa as she added, 'If I hadn't already decided not to have any, this past week would have put me off for good. It'd be like taking your work home with you!'

'Maybe you'll change your mind when you get married,' Lissa suggested, without looking at Hugo.

Jayne was scornful. 'Not me! I'm a career woman. If I marry, it'll be to someone who doesn't want children either.' She too did not look at Hugo, but Lissa felt she was underlining her viewpoint for his benefit and also trying to tell Lissa why Hugo preferred her. He need not feel any obligation to Jayne. He could marry her and feel confident that she wouldn't pester him to have children or leave him if he still felt he couldn't. The dilemma would never arise because Jayne was a career woman.

Jayne said pointedly, 'Where's your boyfriend Paul, Lissa?'

'He was bleeped a while ago. He's on call tonight.' She saw no point in trying to deny the 'boyfriend'. After all, everyone knew that she went out with Paul quite a lot, even if they didn't know it was strictly a platonic relationship.

'He looks like good family man material,' Jayne teased. 'You should cultivate him.'

Lissa was desperate to escape. She couldn't think of anything to say that wouldn't be offensive, and she couldn't bear to look at Hugo. Jayne's remarks were a bit insensitive, given that she must know all about him now.

'I—I must have a word with Warren,' she said hurriedly. 'There's something I've just remembered I want to ask him.'

Jayne smiled, showing pearly teeth, Her relief at getting rid of Lissa was plain. Lissa stole a brief glance at Hugo. 'Enjoy the rest of the party.' Then she fled across the room into a crowd of people.

Supper was over by the time Paul returned. The dancing had started again, and Lissa danced with him. They talked about the two accident victims he had been called to attend to, but Lissa's mind was only half on the conversation. Her eyes darted among the dancers and eventually found Hugo and Jayne. They were talking earnestly and he was holding her close. Jayne's long lashes were fluttering and her gaze was unmistakably adoring.

Paul had noticed too. Grimly he said, 'Anything they can do, we can do better!' And he proceeded to hold Lissa very close, brushing his cheek against hers and kissing her. Instead of protesting, Lissa closed her eyes and tried to imagine that she was in Hugo's arms, as Paul was no doubt imagining he was in Jayne's.

The next day Lissa took over Warren's job on her own. She felt some trepidation as she installed herself in the charge nurse's office, briefed the new shift for the first time and prepared to shoulder the day's responsibilities, its crises and dramas, its highs and lows.

There were discharges to process, parents of elective surgery patients to be contacted, and all of it seemed to require a mountain of paperwork. I'll never have time for any real nursing, she thought with a pang of dismay. But she was too involved to stay off the wards for long, and after the first few days of feeling her way she organised the routine so that she did spend some time with the children, especially new admissions.

There was one new admission that she would rather not have had to make. Toby Foreman came back. His mother brought him in and A & E sent him up straight away to be admitted.

His lip was cut, and when Lissa opened the gown Casualty had put on the boy she nearly gasped aloud. He had several large bruises on the torso and she noticed others that were now fading on his arms and legs.

'How did this happen?' she asked his mother in as calm a voice as she could manage.

Cheryl Foreman looked distraught and her answer was defensive. 'I kept telling him not to play in the street because of the dogs, but he would. This big dog chased him and he fell over trying to get away from it.'

Lissa said nothing except, 'He falls over a lot, doesn't he?'

'Yes, he does. He won't do as he's told.'

Lissa looked at the swelling on the little boy's forehead. It was turning yellow and the skin was broken. He had hit his head against something hard. Footpath? Kerb? She couldn't help speculating. The big brown eyes that looked up at her were apprehensive, but the child did not cry, in fact he made no sound at all. He just seemed to accept what was happening to him.

Lissa tried to coax a smile out of him. 'Well, Humpty Dumpty, if you're going to keep falling over, we'll have to put you together again, won't we?'

He stared at her blankly, and made no response. Smiles did not often form on those cherubic lips.

'Will he have to stay in for a few days?' Cheryl Foreman asked in a low voice, as though she hoped the answer would be yes.

'I think it might be an idea if we keep him under observation,' said Lissa, knowing that was what A & E had recommended.

Mrs Foreman looked relieved. As she flicked her long rather untidy hair over her shoulder, Lissa caught a glimpse of the side of her neck and shoulder and flinched. She pretended not to notice the blue patches she had seen there. 'I can't keep my eye on him all the time,' said Cheryl plaintively. 'I've got the baby. . .'

'I know. Life can be very difficult.' Lissa looked straight at the woman. 'Has the social worker been round to see you recently?' she asked casually.

A stubborn look came into Cheryl's face. 'There's nothing to come for. I look after my children! I'm a good mother,' she added defiantly.

But the trouble is your husband isn't a suitable father, Lissa thought, but did not say. She said again, 'Yes, we'll keep him in for a few days. We'll need to give him a thorough check-up.' She met Cheryl's nervous gaze and guessed that she must be going through a bad patch, and felt unable to protect Toby.

As Lissa expected, Mrs Foreman said she could not

stay with her son, and Toby seemed indifferent to her departure. He was thinner than Lissa remembered, and there were dark circles under his eyes, which had a dull expression. When she picked him up in her arms and spoke soothingly to him, he clung tightly to her, and as she had felt before, she felt now that he was starved of affection.

'That wasn't a dog that did this to you, my love, was it?' Lissa muttered angrily. 'And if someone doesn't do something, you're going to "fall over" once too often. . . Now, let's get the doctor to take a look at you.'

Lissa herself was not in a position to do anything about Toby's unfortunate situation personally. She could only alert others. She voiced her fears to Paul, and to Hugo. Although both agreed with her that the recent comparatively minor injuries to Toby were most probably inconsistent with being chased by a dog and falling over, they said the evidence wasn't conclusive.

'However, dogs don't wear boots,' was Paul's comment.

A few days later Hugo told her, 'I'm advised that the situation is under control.' His expression showed that he was not totally happy about it.

'What can we do?' she asked helplessly.

'Nothing, I'm afraid. It's out of our hands. The psychologists say that a child is better off in his own home, with his mother, than in care. Supervision is continuing in Toby's case.'

'Twenty-four hours a day?' Lissa said bitingly.

'They make unannounced visits. That usually seems to bring about immediate improvements.'

'Yes, which is probably why we didn't see him for a

couple of months, but as soon as they stopped check-ing. . .' She looked at him steadily. 'She was bruised too, Hugo. And frightened. She was so relieved that we admitted Toby. She had nowhere else to take him.'

'Toby's not her husband's child, but the baby is—is that right?'

'Yes.'

'What would you do? Ask for a protection order?'

'Yes,' Lissa said emphatically. 'I don't think he should be allowed to go home this time. It obviously isn't safe.' She took a deep breath. 'He's only three years old, Hugo. A mere baby. Fragile. . .'

Hugo's expression was grave. 'I'll see what else I can do.'

But there was nothing more he could do, it seemed. It was a welfare matter, not a medical one, once the child was well enough to go home, and the situation was under control, he had been told.

A few days later Cheryl Foreman phoned to say she would be coming to take Toby home the next day. She sounded nervous. 'We're going away,' she said. 'My husband's got a job up the country.' Her voice faltered tearfully.

'Don't you want to go?' Lissa asked intuitively.

There was a long silence, then Cheryl said, 'I have to.'

Lissa took a chance. 'You don't have to, Mrs Foreman. You could leave.'

There was another long pause and Lissa thought she could hear faint sobs. Then Toby's mother said in a whisper, 'I—I can't. Where would I go? Besides, he'd—kill me—and the kids. . .'

'Not if you went to a safe place,' Lissa told her.

'I haven't got any money. . .' Cheryl Foreman's voice was low, despairing.

'That wouldn't be a problem. A friend of mine could help you,' Lissa offered. 'She works in a women's refuge. She'd look after you, and he wouldn't be able to find out where you are.'

Lissa waited patiently for the answer. She was hardly surprised when Mrs Foreman said dully, 'Thank you. . .but it'll be all right. He's got a job.'

Why some women stayed with men who bashed them and their children, Lissa still found it hard to comprehend, but this wasn't the first time she had encountered such a situation.

'Well, if you want to change your mind, just let me know,' she said, knowing it was no use trying to persuade the woman. She sounded, Lissa thought, pretty near the end of her tether. 'I'll speak to Dr Norris about discharging Toby. Can you call back later?' And tonight, she decided, she would also speak to Maggie.

Maggie was sympathetic but cautious. 'You're taking the law into your own hands, aren't you, Lissa?'

'Probably, but I've got to stop the poor little kid going away with them. So will you ring Carla for me?'

'Sure. I guess she'll know best how to handle this.'

A few minutes later Lissa had made arrangements with Carla, who was the co-ordinator of a women's refuge, and a clinical psychologist. She was calm and matter-of-fact, and to Lissa's relief agreed to abet her.

The next morning, Lissa waited in some trepidation for Cheryl Foreman to arrive. What if she refused to go with Carla? What if she kicked up a big fuss when she found out that Toby had already gone?

'Surely Paul or Hugo could have done something?' Karyn queried.

She had been in on what was happening when Lissa had taken Toby down to Carla, who was waiting in her car, earlier. Lisa hoped the rest of the staff would assume that he had gone home. There was so much to do in the mornings, no one had time to think about whether something was a bit unusual. And there was nothing too unusual about a nurse taking a patient down to the parent or other relative who had called to collect him.

'They couldn't,' Lissa said. 'It's not a medical matter, so it's out of their hands, and ours. We can only make reports about what we see or suspect. And the social workers have to be careful. They can't make wrongful accusations. Knowing something and proving it are two different things.' She added, 'Don't worry, Karyn, I'll take full responsibility.'

'I just hope you're right and she'll react the way you want her to. If she starts screaming the place down and accusing you of kidnapping her baby. . .' Karyn drew the edge of her hand across her throat. 'You'll be for it, Lissa. Stepping outside the bounds of duty and all that.'

'I know the risks,' Lissa said stubbornly. 'I just hope she gets here before we start having doctors around.'

Carla had returned as promised by the time Cheryl Foreman arrived. To Lissa's relief Mrs Foreman had brought the baby with her. She looked wary and defensive. Lissa took her into her office and introduced her to Carla. She offered them both a cup of tea, then went out to make it in order to let Carla talk to Toby's mother alone. When she returned, Cheryl was saying in a plaintive tone, 'I can't. . . I just can't. He'd kill me!'

And Carla replied in her quiet calm voice, 'You can, and he won't, because we'll look after you. He won't be able to find out where you are. We'll tell him you've left him and you won't even have to speak to him if you don't want to.' She glanced at Lissa, gave a reassuring little smile and with a nod indicated that it would be better if she and Cheryl were left alone for a little longer.

Lissa left them with the tea and busied herself in the ward. Presently Carla came to find her. She was smiling. 'I've convinced her. She's scared stiff, but she's also at the end of her tether. She knows she can't protect the boy, and she's scared that worse might happen to him. She doesn't want to go away with her husband. She had nowhere to go, so she was frightened to leave him before. She'd reached the stage of being unable even to think straight. It's a struggle for her to trust anyone, but I think I have her confidence now.'

'Sometimes there are things I just can't believe,' Lissa said, drawing a hand across her brow, 'and child abuse is one of them.'

'I hope you don't get into trouble over this,' said Carla. 'But you did the right thing. If anyone needed help it's that woman and her little boy. Don't worry, we'll take care of them, and I'll let you know what happens.'

A few moments later, Lissa watched Carla and Cheryl Foreman walk along the corridor until they were out of sight. Her throat felt dry, her stomach cramped. And then, through a haze, there was Hugo looking at her strangely.

'Where's Toby?' he asked as though sensing something was amiss.

Lissa felt herself swaying, and the room swam for a moment. 'Gone home. . .' She muttered.

'Wasn't that his mother I just saw walking down the corridor?'

'Yes.'

'Toby wasn't with her,' Hugo said, puzzled. 'Who was the other woman?'

The tension of the past little while was too much. 'I think I'm going to faint,' said Lissa.

'What's the matter?' He was steadying her, pushing her back into her office and guiding her to a chair. 'Sit down, head between your knees.'

'It's all right, I'm OK now.'

Hugo said gently. 'Hadn't you better tell me about it?'

'Yes,' Lissa said, 'I suppose I had.'

CHAPTER NINE

THE day after the drama of Toby Foreman's unortho-
dox discharge from hospital, Lissa was still feeling
shaky, and somewhat surprised to find herself still
charge nurse at the SCG. What she had done, as Hugo
had pointed out, was against all the rules and probably
deserving of instant dismissal.

When she had recovered a little from her near
fainting fit and was sipping a cup of tea, he had pulled
no punches in telling her exactly what risks she had
been taking.

'You can't just take the law into your own hands,
Lissa.'

Lissa had jutted her lower lip and answered defensively, 'The child's life might have been in danger. I had
to do something.' Tears had suddenly filled her eyes.
'Suppose—that had been the last time? Suppose next
time. . .'

Hugo, leaning against her desk, had bent forward
and clasped her knee. His face had come very close to
hers. 'I know. . . I know why you did it, Lissa.'

'I take full responsibility for what I did,' she insisted.

'That's not the point,' he said patiently. 'Our responsibilities are clearly defined, and if we stepped over the
line too often into someone else's area of expertise, the
result would be chaos.'

Lissa clamped her lips together, biting the inside of
them. 'I know that, Hugo,' she sighed. 'And I wouldn't

normally have done that, but I was *frightened* for that baby.' Her brown eyes were full of mute appeal.

He squeezed her knee comfortingly. 'I'm not really lecturing you, just concerned for you.' He brushed a strand of hair back from her forehead, and his finger-tips lightly trailing across her temple sent rapid signals to her heart. 'You were very brave, Lissa. Braver than the rest of us. You weren't afraid to lay your job on the line.'

She smiled wryly. 'I never even thought about my job.'

'No,' he said softly, 'you wouldn't.'

It had been a wonderful few minutes, sitting there in her office with him, because even though he was trying to be firm with her, she knew that deep down he approved of what she had done.

'I was the one who had the opportunity to do something,' she said. 'I'm sorry, Hugo, but if I'd told you what I intended to do you'd have felt bound to stop me or to refer it to someone else, and I couldn't take that risk.'

His dark eyes were unfathomable as he looked steadily into hers. I love him so much, she thought helplessly. Why can't he love me? If only I could do something more for him, if only I could rescue him as I rescued Toby. . .

'Perhaps I should resign,' she murmured.

'I don't think that's necessary. In fact what's happened need not go any further than here.'

Lissa was grateful. 'Thank you. I think I ought to tell Paul, though.'

His face seemed to harden. 'Yes, tell Paul,' he said.

She wondered if he was jealous because he had realised that Paul was also smitten with Jayne.

She was still thinking about it all the next morning, when Paul arrived. She took him aside and told him what had happened. He whistled low and gave her shoulder an admiring pat. 'What a girl you are!'

They talked about it for a few minutes, and Paul asked where Cheryl Foreman and her children were. Lissa shook her head. 'I can't tell you, Paul, because I don't know myself. Carla said it was better if I didn't know. The locations of refuges are kept secret, for obvious reasons. The fewer people know where they are, the better.'

'I predict that Foreman will be hopping mad when he finds out what's happened.'

'Carla said he would be advised. He was supposed to be going up-country today to a new job. I hope he's gone.'

Later in the morning Paul returned to tell Lissa that they would be transferring a child from the medical ward.

'Osteomyelitis,' he said. 'Of the femur. She's not responding to antibiotics, so Hugo's decided on surgery. I'd like you to chat her up a bit, Lissa. She's pretty down, poor kid, but stoical. She's suffered a good deal of pain and she's anxious about the surgery. She's a country kid and her parents aren't able to stay down here with her—they have a farm. Try and cheer her up a bit, will you? She'll have to be barrier-nursed, so she'll need to be in a room on her own.'

When Kate Denning was comfortably installed in a small room off the main wards, Lissa went along to see her, taking some books and magazines.

'Hello, Kate,' she said brightly. 'So you've come to visit us for a change?' She clasped the child's hand.

'We're going to look after you in Pinocchio for a while until you've had that bothersome old abscess drained.'

Kate's eyes brimmed with tears. 'Are they going to cut my leg off?'

Lissa was appalled. 'No, darling, of course not! Whatever gave you that idea?'

'My brother. He said they'd probably have to chop my leg off, and he laughed. . .he's always laughing at me.'

'He was only joking, Kate love.'

'He said that's why I was going to be moved from the medical ward to surgical. He said this is where they chop people up.'

'Your brother is a very ignorant boy,' said Lissa severely. 'He doesn't know what surgery is all about. Surgery is all about mending people, not chopping them up. Sometimes the surgeon has to have a look inside a part of you to find out what's wrong, and sometimes it means taking out a little bit of tissue like tonsils or an appendix that might be diseased, so it won't hurt you or make you feel ill any more. Sometimes it means mending a broken leg, or repairing a hole in a heart, or even giving somebody a new kidney. In your case it's a very simple operation to take all the pus out of an abscess so that it won't hurt any more or make you feverish. Sometimes we can fix it with medicines, but if we can't then we make a little cut and insert a tube to drain it. A little bit of dead bone might have to be removed too, that's all. As soon as your hip's better, the wound will be stitched up again so you'll hardly know it ever happened.'

'Rodney said you get put to sleep. He said you might wake up in the middle just when the—the scalpel was cutting into you.'

'My word, I'd like to say a few words to your brother!' said Lissa grimly. 'He's just an awful tease, Kate. He doesn't know what he's talking about. . .'

'But Sister does!'

Lissa turned, to see Hugo smiling down at them both. 'A very reassuring description, if I may say so,' he murmured, touching Lissa's shoulder and leaving his hand there for a moment. Lissa blushed. Hugo said, 'Hello, Kate.'

'Hello, Dr Stanfield,' said the little girl. 'When am I going to have my operation?'

'Tomorrow morning.'

'Will it take long?'

'Not very long. You'll wake up very soon afterwards and before you know what's happened you'll be back in bed here. Your hip might be a little bit uncomfortable, but it won't be for long, I promise you.'

'And you won't cut my leg off?'

'Most certainly not!'

'Promise?'

'Cross my heart.' He smiled at the child. 'Believe me?'

The anxious little face relaxed and she smiled. 'All right.'

Hugo followed Lissa back to her office. 'Can you spare a few minutes?' he asked.

'Yes, I think so.' She felt a strange premonition as she looked at his rather grave expression. Perhaps she was in trouble over Toby after all. 'Is something wrong?'

Before he could answer, his bleeper let out a shrill electronic summons. Hugo swore softly, and picked up her phone. As he replaced the receiver after finding out where he was needed, he said, 'I'll be back shortly. Sorry.'

Lissa stared after his departing figure, with a sinking feeling inside that she hadn't heard the last of the Toby escapade yet. But the next development came not via Hugo, but as a complete surprise.

Her thoughts were cut off when the phone rang. A rather anxious receptionist said, 'There's a Mr Foreman on his way up. He seems rather belligerent.'

Lissa started as her door burst open, and a stocky unshaven man of medium height stood there scowling at her. 'Thanks,' she said into the phone. 'He's just arrived.' Slowly she put the phone back on the rest.

'Mr Foreman?' She faced him apprehensively, wary of the rapidly shifting eyes and the aggressive stance he had taken up. As he advanced into the room and closed the door, she began to feel frightened. She hadn't thought that he might come here to make trouble. She should have asked Reception to alert Security.

'Sister Moran?' he growled. 'You're in charge of the children's ward?'

'Children's Surgical, yes. . .'

He leaned towards her across the desk and the fumes of alcohol were strong. 'It was you, wasn't it? You talked Cheryl into it, didn't you? She told me. . . Well now, Sister Busybody, you can tell me where she is.'

Lissa held herself rigid, hands clasped together to stop them shaking. 'I'm sorry, Mr Foreman,' she said in a calm tone, 'I can't tell you that.'

'You better had!' he said threateningly.

'I don't know where she is.'

'Don't give me that! Just tell me where she's gone. Talking her into leaving, who do you think you are, trying to run other people's lives. . .what right have you got. . .?'

'I was afraid for Toby,' Lissa told him.

'Toby! The little brat!'

'You beat him, didn't you?'

Greg Foreman's face was dark and twisted, and the day's beard growth made him look more formidable. 'You be careful what you're saying, Sister,' he said nastily. 'I could sue you for that.'

Lissa was too incensed now to feel frightened. 'Toby didn't get that last lot of cuts and bruises falling over after being chased by a dog,' she said heatedly. 'So I suggest you leave them alone, Mr Foreman. I suggest you go to your job up-country and stay there. Child abuse *is* a crime, you know.'

To her surprise he seemed to crumple a little, and she saw that his hands were shaking. 'Well, maybe I lost my temper and slapped him a bit hard once or twice. . . Trouble with Cheryl is she doesn't discipline the little blighter.' He lifted his chin truculently. 'My old man used to beat the livin' daylights out of me, and no harm done.'

Lissa felt pity for him then. He appalled her, revolted her, but in the shifty eyes there was vulnerability. The victim had once again become the victimiser. People who abused children had most often been abused themselves. The thought that Toby, sweet lovable little Toby, could be caught in the same vicious circle made her want to weep with fury.

She said quietly, 'Mr Foreman, I think you'd better go. Just face the fact that Cheryl has left you. You know why. She couldn't take any more. Don't try to find them.'

The man looked at her for a moment, uncertainly,

and she thought he was going to do as she asked, but suddenly anger flashed into the red-rimmed eyes and he said, 'Bloody do-gooder! Interfering in people's lives. You'll tell me where she is or else. . .'

He caught her by surprise when he made a sudden rush around the desk, reaching for her. Lissa stepped back to escape around the other side, stumbled as she turned and caught the side of her face against the edge of the cupboard which projected from the wall. As the shaft of pain ran up her cheekbone and temple and through her eye, and Greg Foreman, fist upraised, loomed over her, she screamed.

The door flew open and Hugo rushed in. 'What the hell. . .? Lissa!'

He must have been about to come in when she'd screamed. The relief she felt transcended all pain and fear. Thank God he'd returned so soon!

Greg Foreman was only inches away from her and Hugo naturally thought he had struck her. There was a loud grunt as the man was grappled from behind and held in a neck-lock.

'What is this?' Hugo demanded, unceremoniously shoving the man against the wall. 'Who are you?'

'It's all right, Hugo. . .it's Mr Foreman. He thought I could tell him where his wife is, but I can't because I don't know.'

Greg Foreman started to move threateningly towards Hugo, but he was not swift enough. Hugo felled him very effectively and he collapsed into a heap against the wall. Lissa heard him swearing, calling her and Hugo foul names, then the man was weeping, harsh sobs that shook his body convulsively. Lissa, holding her hand over her eye, just stood there, until Hugo said, 'Get out of here, Lissa. I'll handle this.'

She heard herself pleading, 'Hugo, he needs help. . .'

The fury in Hugo's face was almost palpable. 'People who beat up their wives and kids, and then try to intimidate nurses with violence, need. . .'

'He's a victim too, Hugo. And he didn't touch me. I hit my head on the cabinet.'

'You mean he didn't hit you?'

'No. I swung round to get away from him and crashed into the edge of the cupboard.'

'He would have hit you.'

'Maybe. . .'

They were both suddenly conscious of the scared faces of two nurses in the doorway. Karyn said, 'We called for help.'

Help came. Two security men removed Greg Foreman, who put up no resistance. Hugo went with them, and Paul arrived.

'Oh, boy!' he exclaimed, examining Lissa's eye. 'Are you going to have a shiner, Sister!'

'Don't!' she groaned.

'I think you'd better let me attend to it. Come on.' On the way to the treatment-room, he asked a nurse to make Lissa some tea, and a few minutes later she was ensconced in the nurses' room, on the couch, relaxing with the cup of tea. Paul had given her a painkiller and her eye, although puffed up so she could scarcely see out of it, was not feeling too bad.

People kept looking in to see how she was, but when Hugo came, she was alone. He stood over her, looking down at her with his usual unfathomable expression. Then he conducted his own careful examination.

'I don't think you've done any real damage to your eye, but you'd better see the ophthalmologist as soon as you can. If the light's bothering you, we'll cover it for you with an eye-patch. He'll probably suggest that anyway for a day or two.'

'I suppose you think it served me right,' she said humbly. 'That I ought to have foreseen what might happen.'

He sat beside her and held her hand as he might have any small patient's that he was attending. A faint smile hovered on his lips. 'You're going to have one hell of a shiner!'

'That's what Paul said. I haven't been game to look yet.' She added hesitantly, 'What happened? Did you send for the police?'

He nodded. 'Yes, we had to do that. But it's probably unlikely any charges will be laid. Foreman's agreed to have treatment, so he's been handed over to Psychiatry. As you said, the man needs help.'

'It's the old story, I'm sure. He was abused as a child himself.'

'Yes. He went into a kind of maudlin state and, influenced by what he'd been drinking to give him the courage to come here, he spilled a lot of it out.'

'So there's hope for him?'

Hugo shrugged. 'Time will tell.'

'It's so sad, Hugo,' she sighed. 'To think that once he was a little boy, like Toby. . .'

His fingers stroked hers. 'Don't dwell on it, Lissa.' He smiled. 'The daughter of a friend of mine thinks it would be wonderfully romantic to be a nurse, all glamorous and exciting, helping people to get well! I try to tell her that nurses often see the rougher side of life as well. I'm afraid nurses do often face worse hazards than doctors.'

Lissa lifted her shoulders and let them fall resignedly.

'It's part and parcel of the job—a very small part. I wouldn't swap being a nurse for any other job. We have our sad moments and our scary moments, but we have happy times to compensate. In spite of incidents like today, I still think it's the most satisfying profession in the world.'

'I'll tell Kim that.' He was really smiling now, the smile that she would always take a little credit for restoring. Then he said tentatively, 'If you feel up to it, I'd like to talk to you about what I started to earlier.'

'Am I to be on the carpet over this after all?'

'No, no, nothing like that. I've explained everything. It's just that there's something I want you to know before it becomes general knowledge.'

Lissa's stomach suddenly became leaden. I know what he's going to say, she thought, and I don't want him to. He's going to marry Jayne, and I can't bear it. He's going to apologise to me again, maybe even thank me for helping him along the road to being normal again. He's going to expect me to wish him and her well. Why doesn't his bleeper go? *Please let his bleeper go again*!

'That's considerate of you,' she muttered, 'but. . .'

The bleeper remained silent. Hugo said, 'It'll be in the papers in a couple of days, that can't be avoided, but I wanted you to know first.'

Lissa let her mind become numb. She would listen, but not think about what he was saying.

'You can bet your life they'll beat it up as they always do,' Hugo went on. 'They'll call it a break-through, of course, although it's only another theory and not a definitive answer at all. . .'

'Hugo!' Lissa's exclamation was low, and because of

her wrong conclusion, incredulous. 'Hugo, you've found something?'

He lifted a cautionary hand. 'It's significant, yes, but not the whole answer. Not yet.'

Lissa forgot about Jayne. 'You're more excited than you're letting on,' she accused.

'I'm hopeful, that's all.' He leaned towards her. 'In all research, Lissa, there's an element of serendipity. We were following one line of investigation when a side turning appeared. We gambled and took it. What we've done is to open up new possibilities, that's all. Look, it would take too long to explain. I'll let you have a copy of the paper we're publishing—that'll make more sense than what you'll read in the newspaper.'

'Why can't the Press just print the plain facts?'

He shrugged. 'They will, but they'll put it in the sort of language that will tempt the reader to read more into it than is actually there. They'll turn scientific speculation into human-interest news, but they'll cover themselves. Just you count the "mays" "mights" and "possibles"!'

'But if people read more into it than they should, that could be giving them false hopes.'

'I know, but it's also a way of letting people know we're doing something, making progress. It shows we're not giving up, that we're not just wasting money, that we believe we can find an answer eventually. It's a morale-booster for everyone.'

'Well, congratulations, Hugo.' Lissa held out her hand. 'Don't be too modest about it. I'm sure it's a significant achievement.'

He clasped her fingers again. 'Thanks.' And then his bleeper did interrupt, puncturing the sudden silence that had engulfed them. He stood up and crossed to the telephone. A few brisk words, a brief smile in her direction and he was gone again.

Lissa lay back and sighed. She was happy for him. His research had achieved something, and that could only help him personally too. He would feel he was at last expiating the self-blame he had felt because of his daughter's death.

She could see that slowly he was coming alive again. She had felt it that night they had made love, and she'd felt it a few moments ago, even more strongly. He hadn't told her he was going to marry Jayne, but Lissa guessed that the time was coming closer and closer.

Why couldn't he have fallen in love with me? she wished, and derided herself for the foolishness of it. Hadn't she willed him to often enough? In fact until the moment she heard of his engagement to Jayne, or that they were living together, she knew she would still, deep in her subconscious, keep repeating the incantation, love me, not Jayne. It was ludicrous, but she couldn't help it, even though aloud she said, 'I don't believe in miracles.'

Lissa saw very little of Hugo for the next few days. He was busy with the media. She heard him interviewed on radio and briefly on television. She thought he handled the media superbly, never letting them faze him, and answering their questions with modesty, refusing to agree with any bizarre claims and yet giving the impression that good solid work was continuing, that he believed an answer would eventually be found; not necessarily by his team, he emphasised, but definitely by someone. Lissa knew that he was trying to give comfort to those who had lost babies, as he had, while not making irresponsible claims. She felt very proud of him.

And so was Jayne Rossney. Lissa didn't see much of Hugo, but she had to see Jayne every day. The young doctor was ecstatic and showed it. Although she wasn't involved in the SIDS research, she suddenly started saying things like, 'We're really on the map now. . .all the other units will be so jealous!' Lissa supposed it was her intimacy with Hugo that made her say 'we' so often.

CHAPTER TEN

'WELL, what do you think, Paul?' Lissa asked anxiously, looking from the baby girl on the examination table to the doctor.

Paul was frowning in concentration. He held the baby's flexed legs in his palms and, with his fingers and thumbs placed in the correct positions over the great and lesser trochanters, the bony prominences below the neck of the femur, delicately lifted the femoral head into the acetabulum. Lissa heard the slight click.

Paul glanced at her. 'Pretty positive Ortolani sign, wouldn't you say?'

She nodded, and began to talk soothingly to the child, who was becoming a little restive. 'There, there, darling, don't cry. You're all right. . .look, here's Teddy, he wants to whisper something in your ear.' She bent down and whispered as she placed the toy near the baby's ear.

Paul smiled. 'Is that bribery and corruption I hear?'

Lissa grinned. 'On children's wards, you get to be an expert.'

'Well, if you ever chuck it in here, you could always join the Mafia!'

The toddler was hugging her toy and gurgling now. Lissa said again, 'Well?'

'I'd say you're a very observant nurse, Sister Moran. There is definitely congenital dislocation of the hip joint, and it's a bit of luck she was admitted for

177

something else, or it might have gone undetected for some time and been less easy to set right.'

The baby, who was just beginning to walk, had fallen and fractured her right radius. Lissa, when relieving one of the other nurses, had been changing her when she had noticed that one leg seemed shorter than the other and the perineum wider than normal. Realising that a congenital condition might have contributed to the child's falling, she had conveyed her suspicions to Paul.

'Who examined her when she was admitted?' Paul asked.

'Casualty did, of course, and the surgeon who set her arm.'

'And here? It wasn't me, I'm sure.'

'No, it was Jayne,' Lissa told him.

Paul flinched. 'Well, I suppose it's easy enough to miss if you're not looking for it.' He chucked the child under the chin, and wiggled the teddy against her chest. 'So, my lovely, I'm afraid you're going to be in for a fairly uncomfortable time for a while.'

'It'll mean an abduction frame, I suppose?' Lissa queried. 'And then surgery.'

Paul nodded. 'Possibly. There are several ways of dealing with the problem. I shall want John Fullarton to see her as soon as possible.'

Lissa nodded. She had expected the orthopaedic surgeon to be consulted.

Paul asked, 'How's your eye?' He peered into her face, grinning.

'Fine now.' It was still a little discoloured, but Lissa had had no problems. She'd had a clean bill from the ophthalmologist. The worst she'd had to suffer had been some ribbing from her colleagues once the shock of the drama in her office had worn off.

When Paul had gone and she had fed Wendy, Lissa laid the baby back her cot, and gave a small sigh. Wendy was laughing at her now, quite unconcerned about the plaster on her chubby little arm, but she would be less nonchalant about the frog-plaster which might eventually engulf most of her tiny body, or the traction that might be necessary to correct the dislocated hip joint. It was a common enough condition, but often took time to correct, and the small patients became fractious. It was trying for parents too, as children with this condition were usually sent home, returning only for changes of plaster and reassessment every couple of months, and this could continue for a year or more.

'Never mind, darling,' said Lissa, directing the baby's attention to a mobile hanging above her cot. 'At least you're curable.' She lingered until the little girl had settled down for her afternoon sleep, wondering how the parents would take the news. Wendy's mother would be in later to stay overnight, while her husband looked after their other two children.

As Lissa turned to go, she almost bumped into Hugo. For some reason she felt nervous at the sight of him. 'Oh, hello. . . I wasn't expecting you today.'

He held her gaze for a moment. 'Eye OK now?'

'Yes, thanks, no problems.' For a moment she thought he was lifting a hand to touch her face, but he shoved his hand deep into a pocket instead, then said in a gravelly voice as though he had a cold, 'Is this the baby with the congenital hip joint dislocation?'

'Yes. At least Paul thinks so. Dr Fullarton's to see her.'

'Paul told me a few moments ago.'

They walked out of the ward together. Hugo hadn't said why he was there yet. Lissa asked, 'How's it going? You've been rushed off your feet by the Press lately, haven't you?'

'It's been a bit hectic,' he admitted.

'But satisfying, I'm sure, knowing you've really contributed something to SIDS research.'

'It helps,' he answered darkly.

She paused at the door of her office. 'Was there something in particular you wanted, Hugo?' If there was he seemed to have forgotten what it was.

He was looking very steadily at her and after a moment said, 'Yes, there was—is.'

She inclined her head questioningly, and he made a small impatient sound and pushed her through the doorway, closing the door behind them. Lissa was startled, but her eyes barely had time to widen before Hugo's mouth was on hers and he was kissing her with a passion that shocked and perplexed her.

'Hugo. . .please. . .' She muttered, as he drew a breath.

He pulled her hard against him. 'Lissa, it's no good. I'm dying a slow death without you. I'm going crazy!'

'Hugo, this is hardly the time or place. . .'

He dragged his hands through her hair, disarranging it and apparently not caring who might come in. Lissa had never seen him so intense. 'I just spoke to Paul.'

'Yes, you said. About Wendy.'

'About *you*! I had to know how things were between you. You'd given me the impression they were pretty intimate.'

'When did I do that?'

The dark eyes were accusatory. 'I saw you in his arms more than once.'

'Once when I came back to the SCG. A welcoming kiss! Another time I was crying on his shoulder.'

'What about Warren's farewell party? You were looking very rapt that night. He was all over you like a rash.'

'And Jayne was all over you! Paul was crying on *my* shoulder.'

Hugo said fiercely, 'Lissa, I don't want you in anyone else's arms, not Paul's, not anyone's, not for any reason. I want you in *mine*.'

Lissa felt as though the world was spinning. 'I thought we'd talked all this out. And what about Jayne?'

'Jayne? What about her?'

'You can't deny you're very friendly with her.'

'She's a colleague.'

'You spend a lot of time with her. You don't hang around Paul as much.'

'Good God, what an accusation! Jayne's a very young, inexperienced intern. She needs a lot of guidance. I try to give it to her, but that doesn't mean I fancy her.'

'You play golf with her.'

'She goes to the same golf club. I have played a few rounds with her.' He grinned suddenly. 'She isn't half as good as you were after only one round.'

'So you coach her. Do you deny you've ever taken her out?'

'Dated her? Yes, I do deny it. I've had a meal at the golf club with her once or twice. Heavens, Lissa, a man has to be polite to a colleague!' His mouth twitched. 'You're jealous?'

Lissa said haughtily, 'I had the impression from Jayne herself that you were. . .well, intimate.'

He threw his head back and laughed. 'I'm flattered!'

'She has a distinctly proprietorial air where you're concerned. The way she talks about your research, as though she's really in on it. . .'

He cupped her face in his hands. 'Oh, Lissa, how wrong you are! But I think I see what's been happening. Jayne has indulged in a bit of wishful thinking perhaps because I've tried to be helpful to her, but her woman's intuition has told her that my interest lies elsewhere. Maybe that's why she often mentioned you and Paul as though you were about to become engaged. She gave me the impression that you were much more than just colleagues and friends, and you must admit you made no secret of the fact that you often went out with him, and lately you seem to have deliberately given the impression that it's more than that.'

Self-defence, she answered silently. Pride, Hugo, that's all. She said aloud, 'We like the same sports. We're almost always in a group. But why should that concern you anyway?'

'There was no affair?'

'No, never.' She hesitated, then said slowly, 'And you've not been having an affair with Jayne?' Even now she was not totally convinced.

Hugo groaned. 'No! Jayne Rossney isn't my kind of woman, Lissa, surely you realise that?'

'I thought she was very much your kind of woman, and that once you'd. . .once you'd discovered you had feelings again, it was only natural you'd turn to her. She's beautiful, clever, she's right on your wavelength, talks your language. You're both doctors. . .'

He looked exasperated. 'She might be a doctor, but

she's very immature emotionally. She has a lot of growing up to do, and maybe when she does she'll realise what a mistake she made rejecting Paul.'

'Oh. He told you he's crazy about her?'

'Yes. When I asked him how it was between you and him, he told me what you just have, that there's nothing but a casual friendship based on your liking to participate in some sporting activities together. When I was sceptical, he blew up and confessed that he was in love with Jayne.'

'Poor Paul!'

'Poor Hugo,' said Hugo, with a faint smile. 'Jealous for nothing.' He crushed her against him. 'Quick, before someone comes in and interrupts or my bleeper goes. Will you marry me?'

Lissa could only stare uncomprehendingly at him. 'Marry you?'

'Don't look so amazed! You know how I feel about you, and I know you're not indifferent to me. You weren't pretending that night at Maneroo. I tried to believe you were, that it was pity, and that you felt somehow you ought to love me because I was your first lover, but I think I knew it was none of those. I felt terrible rejecting you, but it was still too soon then. I was in love with you but still locked in the past. Lissa, please. . .put me out of my misery, and say yes *now*. I know it's a ghastly way to propose, but I couldn't wait, I had to ask you now, I have to have your answer now. . .or go crazy.'

'What's happened?' she asked slowly. 'I thought you were afraid to marry again. I thought you couldn't bear the thought of having children. I thought an affair with a career woman like Jayne who didn't want children would be safer for you. I thought you didn't want to be

committed, to have obligations. I thought you weren't
prepared to take risks.'

He looked at her for a long searching moment. 'I've
been learning,' he said simply. 'Learning to think and
feel and live normally again. You helped me begin,
and the research helped too. I've stopped being negative. My own common sense has vanquished the
shadows at last. From your friends at Maneroo, from
you, I learned about taking risks, and I'm not so afraid
now.' He smiled tenderly at her. 'Love can make you
strive to come to terms with any problem. When you
screamed and I thought that man Foreman had
assaulted you, injured you, I realised just how important you were to me—that I had to stop grieving or I'd
lose you. I was afraid I already had lost you—to Paul.
Suddenly I knew that, given the chance, I would take
any kind of risk to make the woman who would take
risks for me, as she took risks for others, happy. Taking
risks was part and parcel of the job, you said. I realised
it's also part and parcel of life. Like a fool, I'd tried
not to fall in love with you, but somehow I couldn't
help it. Every time I saw you, I wanted you so much I
ached. . .you seemed to have bewitched me.'

He was smiling, but Lissa suddenly froze.
Bewitched? Had she bewitched him after all? Was he
here now only because of her incantations and spells,
the waywardness of her subconscious willing him to
love her, not Jayne? Had she captured him against his
will? She stared at him. She couldn't believe he really
did want to marry her, and that made her bizarre
thoughts believable.

'Marry me, Lissa.'

His voice seemed to come from a distance, and Lissa
felt a cold clutch of fear at her heart. If she had

compelled him against his will, then it wouldn't last. It was false. He didn't really love her. She had only *made* him fall for her. Oh, why hadn't she let well alone? She had tricked him and would be punished for her presumption.

'I—I can't. . .' She muttered.

Hugo looked shattered. He held her face in his hands. 'Lissa, I love you,' he said in a voice rough with emotion. 'Do you love me?'

She moistened her lips nervously. 'Yes,' she said faintly. She could feel herself weakening, but she went on, 'It—it might not be real. I—we would have to be sure that. . .'

'Sure that what?' he demanded. 'Come on, you little witch, tell me what doubts you have.'

Lissa cringed at that word again. Was she a witch? He would think her a fool. Nevertheless, she said, 'Hugo, did you ever feel compelled to seek me out?'

'All the time, my darling!'

'Even sometimes against your will? You couldn't help yourself?'

He sighed. 'Yes, I would find myself wandering up to the ward on some pretext or other quite often. It was as though you'd hypnotised me.'

'That's sort of what I did.'

Hugo stared at her. 'Is this a joke, Lissa?'

She shook her head vigorously. 'I know this sounds silly, but. . .' In a few shaky words she told him how she had willed him to fall in love with her, and how once she'd started to do it, she couldn't stop.

He broke into incredulous laughter. 'Lissa, are you telling me that you've been putting spells on me, bewitching me, taking over my mind and soul with your witchcraft?'

'I tried not to.'

'You don't believe that it's possible, do you?' he derided.

She shrugged. 'I don't know.'

He gave another loud snort of laughter. 'Lissa! What's come over you? How can you be so unscientific? This is quackery!' He gathered her back into his arms. 'When did you first start weaving your nefarious spells over me?'

'When I came back from England. When I thought you and Jayne. . .'

Hugo looked smug as he asked, 'Why did you come back, Lissa?'

She took a deep breath. 'Because of you.'

He demanded the truth. 'Are you quite sure?'

'I'm afraid so. I knew it was stupid to even imagine you might be interested in me, that it was just foolish wishful thinking on my part because you'd taken me out to dinner and kissed me before I left Melbourne, but I couldn't seem to help myself.'

He was shaking with mirth. 'Did it never occur to you that I might have been willing you to come back? After you left, I felt as though a light had gone out of my life. I had this dream where I went up to the ward and found you back there, so I willed you to come back, and one day it happened. I was never more surprised in my life, or delighted.'

'I thought you seemed quite pleased to see me,' she admitted.

'Pleased? I was overwhelmed! As soon as you'd left, I knew I was in love with you. But I thought there was no future for me with you because I didn't think I'd ever come to terms with marrying again. In spite of my willing it, when you did come back I was scared. My feelings were rushing ahead of me. I knew I had to have more time, that even if you were to fall in love with me I couldn't ask you to take on an emotional cripple. What if I never recovered? There were times, Lissa, when I feared I never would. And you made it clear that you wanted a family.'

'I wanted you more,' she assured him.

He stroked her cheek tenderly. 'You were the only one who really understood.'

'Did you really will me to come back?' Lissa asked with incredulous delight.

'Every day, every night, my lovely. I knew it was a ridiculous obsession, but I couldn't get you out of my head. I didn't believe for one moment that you'd come back. It was a shock to find that you had!' He smiled at her. 'It seems that we've been bewitched by each other.' He paused, then said thoughtfully, 'I suppose if two people are meant for each other, nothing on earth will keep them apart. Wherever they are, whatever they're doing, they will be bound by invisible strings, until eventually they come together. It wasn't spells or hypnotism, Lissa, that drew us together, it was simply that powerful attraction that one person can have for another.'

'You mean it was inevitable we would fall in love, that you can't gain something just by wanting it?'

'Of course you can't. You don't really believe that, do you?'

Lissa smiled a little sheepishly. 'Not really. It's just hard to believe that you love me of your own free will. I mean, there are so many other women more suited to being your wife. . .'

'There is no other woman more suitable for being my wife.' He held her away from him and looked at her anxiously, 'Lissa, I'm not totally cured, but at last I'm trying. I still need time—but with you to help me. . .' He looked doubtful. 'It's so much to ask.'

'Are you changing your mind again?'

'No!' He held her closer, silent for a moment, and then said urgently, 'Now, please answer the question. I'm afraid that any minute now someone is going to come in.'

'What question was that?' murmured Lissa, running her hands up his spine and into his hair.

He breathed against her ear, 'Will you marry me?'

'Oh, yes,' she whispered. 'Oh, yes, please.'

His eyes twinkled. 'You'll have to learn to play golf.'

She smiled. 'And you'll have to learn to windsurf.'

Close to her lips he whispered, 'For you, my darling girl, I'd learn anything.'

'Kiss me, Hugo,' Lissa murmured. 'That's one thing you don't have to learn, and I don't quite believe this yet.'

At the precise moment that Hugo's lips touched hers, his bleeper peremptorily summoned him. The sound jerked them apart. Hugo swore under his breath, then said, 'I'll pick you up at seven this evening. We'll eat at my place. I think we still have a lot to talk about.' His loving look said that talking wasn't all he had in mind.

IN THE SHIMMERING SPLENDOUR OF A GREAT MONARCHY, ONE LOVE BECAME A LEGEND . . .

DEFY THE SUN – Mallory Dorn Hart £3.50

A sudden stolen kiss and the moment was over, yet the memory of that fleeting embrace would burn forever. Julie de Lisle Croixverte, a beautiful widow returning to the dazzling court of Louis XIV to forget her cruel marriage and Nicolas de Courcillon, a noble adventurer loyal only to the King.
In the glittering ballrooms of Paris, the two meet once more and so begins a dangerous web of treachery and intrigue that would seal the promise of their love – or sweep them worlds apart.

December 1990

W●RLDWIDE

4 MEDICAL ROMANCES
AND 2 FREE GIFTS
From Mills & Boon

Capture all the excitement, intrigue and emotion of the busy medical world by accepting four FREE Medical Romances, plus a FREE cuddly teddy and special mystery gift. Then if you choose, go on to enjoy 6 more exciting Medical Romances every two months! Send the coupon below at once to:

MILLS & BOON READER SERVICE, FREEPOST PO BOX 236, CROYDON, SURREY CR9 9EL.
No stamp required

✂ - ✂

YES! Please rush me my 4 Free Medical Romances and 2 Free Gifts! Please also reserve me a Reader Service Subscription. If I decide to subscribe, I can look forward to receiving 6 Medical Romances every two months for just £8.10 delivered direct to my door. Post and packing is free, and there's a free Mills & Boon Newsletter. If I choose not to subscribe I shall write to you within 10 days – I can keep the books and gifts whatever I decide. I can cancel or suspend my subscription at any time. I am over 18.

EP89D

Name (Mr/Mrs/Ms) _____

Address _____

_____

_____ Postcode _____

Signature _____

mps
MAILING
PREFERENCE
SERVICE

Mills & Boon

Discover the thrill of 4 Exciting
Medical Romances – FREE

FREE
BOOKS FOR YOU

In the exciting world of modern
medicine, the emotions of true love
have an added drama. Now you can
experience four of these
unforgettable romantic tales of passion
and heartbreak FREE – and look forward to
a regular supply of Mills & Boon
Medical Romances delivered direct to your door!

❧ ❧ ❧

Turn the page for details of 2 extra
free gifts, and how to apply.

An Irresistible Offer from Mills & Boon

Here's an offer from Mills & Boon to become a regular reader of Medical Romances. To welcome you, we'd like you to have four books, a cuddly teddy and a special MYSTERY GIFT, all absolutely free and without obligation.

Then, every two months you could look forward to receiving 6 more **brand new** Medical Romances for £1.35 each, delivered direct to your door, post and packing free. Plus our newsletter featuring author news, competitions, special offers, and lots more.

This invitation comes with no strings attached. You can cancel or suspend your subscription at any time, and still keep your free books and gifts.

Its so easy. Send no money now. Simply fill in the coupon below and post it at once to -

Mills & Boon Reader Service, FREEPOST, PO Box 236, Croydon, Surrey CR9 9EL

NO STAMP REQUIRED

YES! Please rush me my 4 Free Medical Romances and 2 Free Gifts! Please also reserve me a Reader Service Subscription. If I decide to subscribe, I can look forward to receiving 6 brand new Medical Romances every two months for just £8.10, delivered direct to my door. Post and packing is free, and there's a free Mills & Boon Newsletter. If I choose not to subscribe I shall write to you within 10 days - I can keep the books and gifts whatever I decide. I can cancel or suspend my subscription at any time. I am over 18.

EP90D

Name (Mr/Mrs/Ms) _____

Address _____

_____

_____ Postcode _____

Signature _____